Margaret: Mother of Twins

Also by R. L. Rhyse

Margaret of Greenwich - Margaret and Erika

Margaret at War - Margaret in Tokyo

Margaret and Eve - Margaret and Velda

Margaret and Emily - Margaret and Hillary

Margaret in London - Margaret at Barnard

Margaret at Barnard/Part Two: Deliverance

Margaret in Berlin – Margaret in Manhattan

Margaret and Venla

R. L. Rhyse

Margaret: Mother of Twins
Book Fifteen in the
Margaret of Greenwich® Series

Wyston Books, Inc.

Margaret: Mother of Twins

Wyston Books, Inc.

www.magaretofgreenwich.com

www.wystonbooks.com

R. L. Rhyse

Margaret: Mother of Twins: a novel

Book Fifteen in the Margaret of Greenwich[®] Series

1. Margaret of Greenwich (Fictitious character)
2. Teenage Girls Fiction
Library of Congress Control Number: 2018963476
ISBN 978-0-9991057-8-8
eISBN 978-0-9991057-7-1
Cover Photograph by Juice Images Ltd.
Licensed from Getty Images

BISAC: YAF022000 (Girls & Women)
YAF011000 (Coming of Age)
YAF029000 (Law & Crime)

Successful spying is the skillful manipulating of human failings.

–Margaret

Margaret: Mother of Twins

Chapter 1

Childbirth is rewarded with an instantly changed life and larger-than-life feelings. The brain rush of never having enough time and especially not for yourself. Having become a mother whose life belongs to their baby, which is where this chronicle begins. Though barely twenty, I had just become responsible for a large, inherited house and newborn twins.

I'm not looking for sympathy since many single parents have it worse. I don't have money problems and when I need a break, there are nearby relatives to watch my babies. Both my mothers would happily steal them too!

"Mothers" isn't a mistype since I do have *two*: an adoptive mother who brought me up and a biological mother who I first learned of as a teenager. I also have a step-mother in Germany but I'll get to that later.

Beginning in high school, writing became my escape and I try to do it daily. Presently, this isn't a problem since my babies sleep a lot. When they're older and need continual watching, I don't know when I'll be able. Which isn't now since their cries indicate that breast-feeding time has arrived.

Chapter 2

My poor sleeping couldn't be blamed on my babies who had fewer problems and slept far better. What kept me awake was the dilemma of what to do with my life.

Returning to Barnard College *was* possible. Fearing a backlash, they wouldn't try to expel me as they had a former dorm-mate when her pregnancy showed. Their excuse, that it was best for mother and child, didn't fool anyone and they backed down upon meeting a storm of protest. But I had outgrown college party life, sometimes feeling fifty from the stress of mothering.

Still, I was heartened by the life of my biological mother, Lena. After being expelled from high school for selling marijuana, she ran away to Texas, supporting herself by doing office work at an escort service. This was followed by a job in Europe where she had simultaneous affairs with two men: a British spy, Peter, in Brussels; and a retired Russian general, Vladimir, in Berlin. Either might be my father since a paternity test was never performed. They know of the situation, get along well, and even work together.

Both wealthy and pregnant with me, Lena returned to America. There followed two widowhoods and her purchase of Greenwich's psychiatric hospital which she manages when not lecturing as a business guru.

"You're not meant for a traditional life," my best friend, Erika, advised me.

"It's hard being a single-parent," I objected.

"You'll manage it. Think what you accomplished in Berlin and London," she said, supportively.

Margaret: Mother of Twins

"Some events are best forgotten," I said.

"I also get depressed when fixating on problems so I don't do it," Erika said, nodding.

I couldn't argue with that logic.

Chapter 3

When a child, my father told me that it takes a strong person to admit they need help. I remembered this when making my decision though being unsure what this comprised.

I sensed that my decision of whether to work or return to school would resolve itself. One path would seem more comfortable and I would choose it. But I lacked confidence to survive as a single parent. Once again, Erika provided the solution.

"A support group helped Hillary after her mother was murdered. Why not try one for single parents," she suggested.

"They'd be older and not see me as an equal," I objected.

"OK, then start your own," Erika replied.

That's where the matter stood until, a week later when feeling *really* depressed, I resolved to do it. And Erika, who is so good at organizing that she must have special genes for it, took over.

"You'll meet at my dad's Manhattan apartment. You could certainly find other single women with similar problems in the City," Erika said.

And that's what happened.

I decided to hold the meetings on Saturday when the City's subways and busses aren't crowded. I didn't expect the others to travel in a chauffeur-driven SUV, as Erika traveled and I when with her.

Chapter 4

The only thing I knew about a support group is that it's more than two people. But Erika had been creating groups since high school.

"You first decide how large it will be and then its purpose," Erika advised.

"Well?" she pressured.

"Seven or eight?" I asked.

"That's a good number. Too large would make it unwieldy. Now, who will be its members?" she asked.

"Young women," I said, more firmly.

"OK, and...?"

"Who feel lost," I said.

"Why do they feel lost?"

I gave Erika a blank look. Creating this group took more planning than I thought.

"Can I make a suggestion?" she asked, tactfully.

"Please do."

"The women feel lost because their lives have changed *too* quickly. Helping each adjust could be the group's purpose," Erika said.

"That's brilliant!" I exclaimed.

"Well, maybe a bit," Erika said, with feigned modesty.

"Where could we find the members? I can only think of one other," I said.

"Who?"

"You, of course, as helper or whatever you want to call yourself," I answered.

Erika has a busy schedule. Besides being a student at Yale, she has a diabetic boyfriend, a new step-mother and family, and helps in her father's business. She then revealed another motive for suggesting this group.

"I'd like Jenna to be in it," she said.

This surprised me. Jenna, Erika's new step-sister, had recently been rescued from a sex-trafficking gang. During her ordeal she was repeatedly raped. Though discharged from Greenwich's psychiatric hospital, she was still fragile. Could she stomach the turmoil of a free-wheeling group? When I asked, Erika's reply was firm.

"We *must* help her," she said.

Chapter 5

I couldn't refuse Erika's request since we had long been like sisters. I would never snub her vital wish and she is the same with me. Still, Jenna *was* fragile, a condition which seemed belied by her beauty. Men stared as she strolled Greenwich Avenue and would have done more were it not for the glaring hulking bodyguard accompanying her, an inescapable companion for members of Erika's billionaire family as Jenna now was.

"I already asked her about the group and she wants to come," Erika added.

This changed my attitude.

"She'd be a good member. Few have experiences as bad but she probably wouldn't want to talk about them," I said.

"Who knows?" Erika said.

We left it at that.

"Seven or eight members would be a good size," Erika said.

"OK," I agreed, letting her take the lead.

"There should be a mix of those doing well and those not doing well," Erika replied.

I wasn't sure how to distinguish them and so simply nodded.

"Those with different situations but not so different that it would be hard to learn from each other."

"Jenna's experiences would be very different from the other's," I objected.

"That's why she'll be my assistant," Erika said.

"OK," I repeated, as my confusion increased.

"It'll work," Erika assured me.

I just smiled, as one does when it's pointless to say anything. When you know someone well, not everything need be talked about. Despite my misgivings, the group *did* work though not as either of us could have expected.

Chapter 6

I let Erika work out the group's details and tried to relax. I had just adjusted to a big change in my life. Not the birth of my twins for which I had months to prepare, but for the unexpected coming of their au pair.

I hadn't planned to have one. What twenty-year-old mother would? But birthing two large babies for three-and-a-half-hours had taken a toll on my body and particularly on its no-longer-private parts. There was so much soreness and bleeding that ordinary things like sitting and urinating and sleeping became problems.

My doctor assured me this was normal. "The body must rid itself of the blood and tissue inside the uterus. It'll taper off. Consider it a heavier period," she said.

She advised me to drink plenty of water and eat high-fiber foods. Most of all, to take it easy, which is how Ingrid entered our lives. Two days after I complained to my German father, Ingrid was hired as my au-pair with my acceptance being a given.

"You'll need help if you're to manage the company's East Coast office," Vladimir had insisted on the phone.

I agreed and thanked him, knowing that he was right. Besides having my best intentions at heart, one doesn't readily argue with a father who is a former general. Still, being the same age as the au pair, I feared that our relationship would prove awkward until Erika advised me.

"One must begin correctly with an employee. Early on, lay down the rules: their pay, working hours, time off, and your expectations. Being firm will allow her to accept you as the boss without resenting your similar ages."

"Huh," I said, not yet having rid myself of this juvenile verbal habit.

Though being friends for nearly half our lives, I still found myself amazed by Erika's management skill.

Chapter 7

I did as Erika advised. While my mother babysat the twins, Erika and I met Ingrid's flight at Newark Airport. While seated in the SUV, I began my questioning.

I didn't doubt Ingrid's credentials since Vladimir would have checked them. But I lacked such basic information as whether she could drive and was fluent in English. I wanted my children to grow up bilingual but English would be their primary language.

Ingrid's crisp English answers reassured me.

"I have an ear for language. My father is a diplomat and I attended Mayfield School during the four years we lived in England. It's a boarding school in Sussex, fifty miles from London."

"You won't drive much for me and maybe not at all. But just in case, do you have a driver's license?" I asked.

"I got an IDP, International Driving Permit, before leaving Germany. It's good for one year and can be renewed," Ingrid replied.

Silence filled the car until she spoke again.

"How old are your twins?" she asked.

"Three months, James and Donna," I said.

Then, because Ingrid looked expectant, I added more. It can be hard for new mothers to stop talking about their children but then wasn't the time. The more about them that Ingrid knew, the greater help she could provide me.

"They're perfect kids, sleeping through the night and eating well. I love them to death but watching them every minute wears on you. Apart from their basic care, your only duty will be to talk to and play with them. There'll be no housework or other chores that some au pairs must do.

"You'll get weekends and two evenings free. You'll get twelve-hundred dollars a month, and if we go on vacation you'll come along. How does this sound?" I asked.

"Very generous," Ingrid replied.

Erika smiled. I had also followed her instruction that a well-paying employer has the most satisfactory workers.

Chapter 8

While our ride home was peaceful, Ingrid's introduction to my babies wasn't. They screamed the moment that I handed them off, which Erika explained. Thanks to her years of therapy, she is my expert on behavior.

"A month-old infant already distinguishes between their mother and others. As soon as they're used to Ingrid, all will be fine," she said, supportively.

Within an hour it was. We became a functioning family in my less than accommodating home.

All houses have personalities. While the one that I inherited had awaited me, it was unfinished. During the years that it was rented, its furniture had been in storage. Re-installing each piece to its original location, as I remembered these, seemed to grant the structure its hungered-for permanence. Its popular Colonial style dated to the 1700s and possessed a peace which I hoped for my family.

The house is a symmetrical two-and-half stories high, rectangular in shape with an elaborately decorated front door. An identical number of windows on the first and second floors flank the entranceway. It has decorative window shutters, paired chimneys, a gabled roof, and a covered porch.

Before we moved in, my adoptive father, who had formerly been a lawyer and became a judge, had ordered its exterior repainted, bathrooms added, and the plumbing and electrical systems modernized. That this extensive work was accomplished within two months reflected the many tradesmen who owed him favors for his years of free legal services.

The house now has six bedrooms and four-and-a-half bathrooms. I plan to have a garage constructed, one keeping with its Colonial style.

While I love my home with its grand wooden staircase, stained glass windows, moldings and built-ins, Ingrid might not. Some furnishings came from my Mormon forebears in Utah. The steer skull and ancient medical artifacts are an acquired taste. Though these reflected my heritage, I could almost hear the house whisper, "Make it yours." Which I intended to do.

Chapter 9

I expected for Ingrid's presence to calm me but it didn't. She made me even more nervous than I had been since I now had *three* kids to worry about.

Ingrid was the youngest in her family. She had been babied by her parents, three sisters, and one brother. She was pretty, sweet, and all that a teenage boy could want in a girlfriend. Unfortunately, she wasn't much help as a babysitter. Still, I couldn't simply return her as one did a poor purchase.

"Consider her a new employee who must be trained," Erika advised.

I did teach Ingrid and her skills improved. She soon diapered the children correctly and I trusted her to bathe and dress them. With me watching, of course.

But I didn't feel completely comfortable leaving them alone in her care, which was the point of her hiring. When going on an errand where I couldn't take them, I asked my mother to babysit.

One of those days arrived quickly. Thanks to Facebook, the membership of my support group grew to eight including Erika, Jenna, and me. One woman lived in a good neighborhood on West Twenty-Second Street, three lived on Manhattan's posh Upper East Side, and the other lived downtown near the South Street Seaport. Erika chose those who seemed compatible. Her logic was, as usual, inescapable.

"People won't change their lives without some degree of financial security. They can't worry about survival too," she insisted.

Margaret: Mother of Twins

There were two single working women, one soon-to-be divorcee, and two widows with ages ranging from twenty-three (her husband had been a Marine officer who was killed in Afghanistan) to thirty-eight (her husband, a software engineer, had died in a car accident).

Though meeting at Erika's pricey Manhattan apartment, I feared that our group would have the feel of the support groups that one reads about, those located in rooms with uncushioned plastic chairs, worn carpeting, and glaring fluorescent lighting. But it didn't.

Chapter 10

It's hard to feel cheerless in Erika's apartment. Though owned by her father and designed by a professional, Erika's decorative ideas prevailed. She had wanted it as her father's respite and workplace, with both activities blending seamlessly.

Here, his home-office contained the latest technology enclosed by 19th century furnishings to harmonize with the historic elegance of The Dakota apartment house. But the room where we met held a comical Banana lamp and Hot Dog sofa. While originally intended as a servant's quarters, its small size forced a physical intimacy which I hoped would develop into an emotional one.

"Humor and insight reduce tragedy and open a new path on life's journey," Erika's therapist had said, when she sought his advice about my group.

"How should we begin?" I asked Erika.

"We should start with food, an inescapable human need. Though not by cooking together since they haven't yet bonded. Setting out ordered-in food would create an initial sense of togetherness," she suggested.

We dressed casually for this meeting, in jeans with a turtleneck or shirt. Erika's outfit, as befit a billionaire's daughter, was expensive: a Veronica Beard Debbie Teal Tux Striped Skinny Jean, "a bargain at two-hundred-ninety-eight-dollars in Richards," she said. Richards is the iconic Greenwich store where residents shop. Erika is a *serious* shopper.

All arrived within ten minutes of each other and our scheduled time, casually dressed in shirt and jeans or exercise clothes. They were pale with the look of a vacationer who took the wrong street and hesitated asking directions.

I had awaited them anxiously, wondering if any would come. Now, with the stage set and players assembled, I began directing.

"Being Scandinavian, Jenna has suggested that we name our meeting *The Blenda Group. Blenda* was a long-ago Swedish warrior who won her battle and so will we," I said.

With these words, their faces seemed to brighten though I might have imagined it.

"I've got a war going on inside me and could use some help," Enid said.

Chapter 11

The sliced turkey, cold salmon, cheeses, and bagels went untouched as eyes focused on Enid.

"Maybe you should tell us something about yourself first," I suggested.

"You're right," Enid said, with a nod. "How can you help me unless you know who I am."

"How confidential is what we reveal?" Joanne asked.

Only then did I study them. Apart from their interest in the group, they seemed to have little in common. Their clothes ranged from inexpensive to designer and their makeup ran the gamut from carefully applied to none. Their sole commonality was living in Manhattan.

One of the women was Oriental and the rest were Caucasian. I didn't know their religion but this isn't important to most City residents. Money is, it being an expensive place to live.

Though not a lawyer, I felt comfortable answering Joanne's question. My father had often discussed his law practice before being elected a judge of Connecticut's Supreme Court.

"Legally speaking, there should be no more expectation of confidentiality here than there is between friends. What is shared should depend on how much trust develops though I suggest that you not reveal private business matters or anything that could place you in legal jeopardy. I wouldn't lie for anyone in court," I said.

Thoughtful expressions appeared on all faces but it was Enid who spoke.

"That's not what frightens me. Just *knowing* some things could be dangerous," she said.

Chapter 12

Enid was correct. After learning *some* information, civil behavior can disappear with life being lost. But we're in Manhattan, not Afghanistan. What could happen here? I asked myself.

"What type of situation are you thinking of?" Jenna asked.

Having been rescued from sex traffickers, her survival antennae were always on high alert.

An uncomfortable silence hovered as we awaited Enid's response.

"My married lover won't leave his wife no matter how much he loves me," she said, finally.

"Is it something religious?" Vera asked.

"No, it's a cultural thing. Having a mistress is OK in his society but not divorce. It could be...messy," Enid said.

Now, *my* security antennae rose as I sensed what concerned Enid. A group where having a mistress is OK but not divorce, and deadly secrets are common. I knew where and so do you if you saw the movie classic, *The Godfather*. Surely the others, except possibly Jenna who grew up in Finland, had made this association too.

"Do you intend to break up with him?" I asked.

"I don't know. My therapist encourages this but my boyfriend helps me. He knows everybody and there's never a problem getting anything whether it's a restaurant reservation or theater tickets or even a doctor's appointment. And he makes me feel secure since no one would dare harm me. He's twenty-seven-years older so the relationship has no future but I don't feel I can leave him. I'm grateful to him for rescuing me."

"Rescuing you?" Joanne asked.

"From the guy who was beating me," Enid replied.

We understood.

Chapter 13

Enid's confession had a boarding-up effect. No one spoke and I feared that no one would. *Another* flop after weeks of failure, I told myself. Looking down on my top, I saw what seemed to confirm this: a chocolate-colored stain which is familiar to every new mother but not something that you would lick off.

"Now would be a good time for the rest of us to describe why we're here. I'll start," I said.

I decided that, by speaking first, the others wouldn't feel they were being placed on the spot. It worked and all visibly relaxed.

"Being the new mother of twins isn't why I need help. I must decide something which will forever change my life and can't do it."

Their absorbed stares drove my words.

"I should be starting my third year at Barnard. Dropping out of college isn't something I'm proud of and I'll murder my kids if they do. But I don't like driving into Manhattan and going back and forth by train and subway isn't realistic. I'm still sore down there."

"Could you afford to live in Manhattan?" Krystal asked.

"Yes. I inherited money along with a house," I explained.

This wasn't true but confessing my theft of twenty-three-million-dollars in Berlin wouldn't be smart. Not to them or anyone.

This impressed them. Money has that effect in New York City.

"What *is* your problem?" Krystal asked, hoping to speed things along.

"I've been offered a job which I'm unsure whether to take," I said.

Chapter 14

After blurting out my dilemma, I became tongue-tied.

Recognizing this, Erika asked Samantha to describe her problem next.

Samantha ("call me Sam") was a Barbie-figured woman of twenty-three. She wore form-fitting black jeans and a tight sweater emphasized her pointed breasts. Her lipstick and nails matched her red hair. As a fellow red-head, I felt the immediate kinship that red-heads have for each other.

Nothing in Sam seemed out-of-place and she looked so put-together that I wondered why she was here. If wearing a mask, her's was a good one. But after learning her story, I realized that she *did* belong with us.

"I have a roommate, Anna. She's thirty-six and an engineer. The apartment is her's, near the South Street Seaport. I can't afford to live there alone and was lucky to find it. Otherwise, I'd be living in a bug-infested tenement and waitressing nights and weekends to pay the rent. I have a huge student loan and beginning editors aren't paid much.

"She charges me nine-hundred dollars a month for a large bedroom and private bath. We share the kitchen and I can use the rest of the apartment when she's away. She travels a lot and I sometimes don't see her for weeks."

"That's low rent for what you're getting in Manhattan," Krystal said.

"I know and don't want to rock the boat. Anna only demands that no one sleep over or I have a party loud enough to cause conflict with the neighbors. I wouldn't do them anyway," Sam said.

"The situation sounds great. What's your problem?" Krystal asked.

Sam seemed to brace herself before speaking. It was as if she feared that describing her worry would change it from a possibility to a certainty. She swallowed hard before speaking.

"I think...it's just possible...that my roommate is a terrorist," Sam said, in barely above a whisper.

Chapter 15

No American can forget the 2001 terrorist attack on New York's World Trade Centers. Many remember what they were doing when it happened and youth became seared by this talk and the wars flowing from it. So, once again, a story had shut us up.

Though fearing what came next, I turned toward Vera. She had been composed, listening calmly as the disasters unfolded. But her tale also didn't come easily. As the group leader, it was my task to encourage the others so I revealed a little more about myself.

"I'm adopted. My worst moment was when I feared that my biological mother would die before we could share what was needed."

This turned out to be the right thing to say. Vera was a widow and the death of a spouse is hard to bear.

"My husband was killed two months ago, thirty-seven days after we returned from our honeymoon," she said, in a flat voice.

We had barely registered what Vera said before she continued.

"Tony was a Marine officer, training government forces in Afghanistan. A suicide bomber killed him and eleven rookie policemen during their graduation ceremony. America is losing interest about such news so this was a one-day item, getting the same space as a wreck which is what that war is. Tony thought this too but soldiers follow orders. Strategy is made by those safe at home."

Margaret: Mother of Twins

Her cynicism was understandable and none of us disagreed. Joanne, who sat beside Vera, touched her hand supportively before speaking.

Chapter 16

Joanne's ironed jeans complemented her business-cut blond hair and wire-rimmed eyeglasses. Her large eyes were made to appear wider by well-drawn eyebrows. Her first words brought us up sharp.

"My husband's death wasn't honorable. He killed himself and maybe because of me," she said.

I dropped my half-eaten sandwich onto the plate.

"He was a forensic accountant, a partner in one of the Big Eight firms. We led a comfortable life and had two good kids. They're in high school and feel lost like me."

Sam asked what I considered an unseemly question.

"Why did he kill himself?"

"Who knows? Why does any alcoholic do what they do?" Joanne asked rhetorically, with a shrug.

"He had a drinking problem since college. Things rapidly went downhill after he arrived drunk for a client conference. The firm pushed him out when he started using drugs too.

"He made his suicide easy for me. It was a snowy night and his car was believed to have skidded into a tree without him wearing a seat belt. The five-million-dollar insurance policy was paid quickly. They say that time makes a difference but it doesn't though on some days I'm fine before going backward," Joanne said, wiping away a tear with her hand.

"If the driving conditions were bad, how can you be sure that his death was a suicide?" I asked, trying to be supportive.

"Because he left detailed notes to help me cope afterward. It's ironic that in the end his meticulousness returned. I might have noticed how troubled he was if I'd been less involved with the kids and my career," Joanne concluded.

None of us could think of anything to say to reduce her feeling of guilt.

Chapter 17

Thirty-four-year-old Krystal was the best dressed of all. Her black lace jumpsuit was a Herve Leger, "at least seven-hundred-dollars," Erika later informed me. Krystal's black leather Derek Lam ankle boots cost another eight-hundred-dollars. She fit in well on Manhattan's Upper East Side and would in Greenwich.

Because her baby-sitter was ill, she had brought her seven-year-old daughter, Kari, who was kept amused by teaching the Uno card game to Erika's bodyguard. "She likes to teach and to win," Krystal said.

Being poised and with an apparently angelic child, I wondered why Krystal needed help. She quickly came to the point.

"I've been a parent for seven years and hate it," she said.

I looked around the room and wondered if the others had the same thought: it's good that her daughter isn't close.

"You hate being a mother?" I asked, trying to keep my voice level.

"No, not that. Kari is a perfect child. She's smart, has tons of friends, and excels at everything she does. I graduated college at nineteen and she may beat that. It's being a single parent that I hate. After separating, my longest relationship was two months."

"That's not necessarily your fault. Manhattan men are a class of asses unto themselves," Joanne said.

"You won't get an argument from me," Enid agreed.

Smiles erupted and I felt pleased. Our group was beginning to bond.

Chapter 18

All eyes turned toward Jenna who had become increasingly nervous as the others spoke. Knowing of the group obligation to share why they were here and fearing the arrival of her turn.

I shot Erika the unspoken question of whether I should intervene and she shook her head "no." Give Jenna time for she's stronger than she looks, Erika seemed to say, and I did.

Jenna did pull herself together.

"I don't like being around people but wasn't always like this. I was once sociable, before being raped hundreds of times," she said, then grew silent.

Eyes widened with disbelief. She must be crazy, the others thought. Just as I would had I not known her story. *Now* be supportive, I ordered myself.

"It's true! Jenna was rescued from European sex traffickers. She's here because of that and is Erika's step-sister," I said.

Attitudes instantly changed to compassionate as experiences were silently compared. Nothing, not even widowhood, was worse than what Jenna endured. The hush that descended over the room ended with my suggestion to Jenna.

"Tell us about it," I encouraged.

"It's like you probably imagine," Jenna began, speaking in a matter-of-fact tone. "After being kidnapped, I was sold to a gang and became one of their stable. We were raped and beaten and starved.

"A person will do anything to survive and I did. A few of us couldn't and killed themselves. On some days, I thought they were the lucky ones."

A shocked silence ensued and Enid faced Jenna.

"I'm glad that you're here. Events that've been burned in memory aren't easy to talk about and I didn't intend to speak of mine. I was trafficked too, though less than you and probably beaten less too. Now I feel better. When words fail, just being with caring people is enough to make life feel worth living again."

Chapter 19

Erika indicated the buffet table and I nodded agreement. There had been enough sharing for our first meeting and downtime was needed. Moreover, I worried about my babies. Though I trusted my mother with their care, they were mine and would miss their mother. How much more they missed me was shown each time I returned.

Our conversation became casual, of shoe sales and similar stuff. All had closed down emotionally, wanting to leave and recover.

"It went well," I said, on the drive back to Greenwich.

"Better than I expected," Erika said.

Jenna said nothing. She wasn't a big talker and the meeting seemed to have worn her out.

My babies *did* miss me, bellowing at my appearance and from hunger too.

My second bonding that day was with my mother. Living in *my* home and becoming a mother had changed our relationship. We were now equals despite my submissive attitude. No matter the age or circumstance, one's parents will always be their parents.

"How is dad?" I asked.

My father had recently been elected to the Connecticut Supreme Court. While closing his law practice had been wrenching, he looked forward to following in the footsteps of his great grandfather who had been a Chief Justice of the Connecticut Court of Appeals.

I had wondered if, as a judge, he would relate differently and was reassured by my mother's reply.

"He's the same though people behave differently. They're hesitant to make casual remarks, as if he might have them jailed on a whim."

I smiled. Knowing my father, he was probably the most tender-hearted judge on the Court.

"How is our new mother?" my mother asked.

I checked that Ingrid, the au pair, wasn't within hearing distance before letting it out.

"*Oh, mom, I don't know!*" I confessed, with greater emotion than intended.

Chapter 20

"I try and try but never seem to be *it*," I moaned.

Seating herself and motioning for me to do the same, my mother asked, "What is *it*?"

"The mighty single parent who can marvelously cook and bake. The community minded mother who raises vegetables and relishes recycling and is always present and caring. The *perfect* mother," I said.

"Could these unrealistic ideas spring from being an adoptee? The foolish thought that you weren't good enough for your mother and must now convince your babies that you'll never abandon them?" my mother asked.

I would have fallen down had I not been seated. Her interpretation and my ensuing insight hit me so powerfully that I *knew* it to be correct.

"All yearn for the perfect family though none ever achieve it. And there's nothing wrong with that though you shouldn't carry this burden. Being human, even your best efforts must fall short. Accept this rather than wasting energy trying to ease your guilt at being imperfect.

"Being a single parent is harder than coupled parenting. Not only must you do everything but you can't make trade-offs with each parent alternating from good guy to tough boss. And you'll have another problem."

"What's that?" I asked, already feeling overwhelmed.

"If you and Randy don't marry soon, when they're older, your kids will fear that you might abandon them for him and you'll have to work this out with them," my mother advised.

"Isn't there *anything* enjoyable about being a parent?" I asked, in a pleading tone.

"Yes, lots. Especially when your kids hug you and say you're the best."

And that's just what I did and what I said.

Chapter 21

After my mother left, I picked up my babies and rejoined Erika. Sprawled and sunning herself on the swinging settee, she sat up to give me room. I handed my daughter to her and held my son. Both children snuggled close.

"That was unexpected," Erika said.

Having long been as close as sisters, I knew that she referred to the group meeting without having to spell it out.

"It was a shocker. I was almost afraid what would come next. I'd expected to help each other with parenting and relationships, not a terrorist and Mafia boyfriend."

"I wouldn't bet on terrorism. Sam's roommate sounds splendid. If seeking a reasonable rent, traveling a lot, and demanding that there be no loud parties or sleepover guests make her a terrorist, the City would be better off with more people like her," Erika said.

"We can't be sure. There may be more to come," I argued.

"It would have been more accurate for Sam to describe her landlord as being *private* than 'a terrorist,'" Erika said.

The kids began fussing, perhaps from the tone of our conversation. We spoke softly to them and they dozed off.

"We'll see," I said, amiably.

The shaded sun and warm bundle in my arms made me sleepy. As my eyelids closed, Erika's statement shook me awake.

"Ingrid has a boyfriend," she said.

"Huh?"

I hadn't yet rid myself of this detestable verbal habit.

"He's *at least* ten years older," she added.

"How do you know?" I asked, feeling annoyed.

It seemed unfitting that Erika knew more what went on in my home than I did.

"Jenna saw her on one of her walks."

Jenna's trauma had turned her solitary. She spent hours wandering Greenwich, lunching in a different restaurant each day.

"What will you do about it?" Erika asked.

"Why should I do anything? She's an adult," I said.

"Jenna said the guy looked like trouble and she should know after what she went through," Erika replied.

Chapter 22

Dealing with Ingrid's dating was an additional problem that I didn't need. But I felt confident, having successfully helped my brother with his girlfriend. Ingrid's confused relationship couldn't be worse than his, I thought. Still, I hesitated.

Ingrid and I were the same age. I was her employer, not her parent, and from a different culture too. Yet I felt that I had no choice. She lived in my home to which she had a key. An unsavory boyfriend placed my family at risk.

I feared, despite her age, that my conversation with Ingrid would resemble those with a child or that she would lie. Love arouses many feelings and some aren't rational. While the children napped, conflict boiled within me.

Thus, as people tend to do, I put off this essential conversation using the usual excuses: Ingrid's infatuation might be brief and nearly over; perhaps Jenna misread what she saw; maybe, if feeling insulted, Ingrid would abruptly return to Europe and leave me in the lurch. Despite her limitations, she was a godsend since my mother wasn't always available to babysit.

Ingrid's smile and obvious joy upon arriving home placed me at ease. Our conversation needn't be now or possibly ever, I decided. While we snacked on the bread pudding that my mother had brought, I spoke of the furnishings I wanted to buy to make the house truly mine.

"Do you need anything for your room?" I asked.

"A double-size bed would be nice," Ingrid said, sweetly.

Margaret: Mother of Twins

I smiled until an unpleasant thought hit me. Ingrid was barely five foot three inches. Why did she need a larger bed?

Chapter 23

A new mother doesn't have time for idle thinking. She has too much to do, particularly after giving birth to multiples. Moreover, I had other worries besides Ingrid. My group, which I had expected to deal with issues of parenting and work, had switched into talk of a terrorist landlord and Mafia boyfriend.

There was also the problem of my babies' father, Randy. While vowing fidelity, what if we didn't marry? I forgave his one affair but wouldn't another. Was it healthy for our children to see him as their occasional sleepover father if he might leave?

These unpleasant thoughts continued until being interrupted by my phone. The call was from Ulrika, the live-in girlfriend and mother of Vladimir's young daughter.

"Your father wants to see you. His plane lands in four hours at Newark Airport," she stated, in a business-like tone.

"Is everything alright?" I asked.

Vladimir had suffered a mild heart attack several years earlier and I became a health worry-wart after a childhood illness.

Ulrika picked up my concern.

"No, his health is fine and our daughter has given him a new lease on life. The company needs an East Coast office and your decision about managing it."

"Oh."

"*Will you*?" Ulrika asked, pointedly.

"I'm not sure but sense that the decision is coming," I said, cautiously.

"He needs your help and believes that you need the outside activity," Ulrika pressed.

Without further deliberation, the decision burst from me.

"I do feel swamped as a mother but at loose ends too. I'll tell him 'yes' when I see him.'"

Ulrika exhaled with relief before changing the subject.

"How is Ingrid working out?" she asked.

"I'm less sure about that," I said.

Chapter 24

"What did she do *now*?" Ulrika asked, in a weary tone.

"You sent me a lemon?" I asked, calmly.

My voice lacked anger since Ulrika had done many favors for me.

"Ingrid's personality is more New York than Berlin."

"Huh?"

"Yes. Germany has a tradition of public manners but Americans, and particularly New Yorkers, are brassy and wild. Which is probably best for kids. Wouldn't most parents prefer outgoing children than submissive ones?" Ulrika asked.

"Yes."

"Just so. Ingrid is more teenager than adult. Lusty and vital, she's growing into her own. Better than being apathetic and uninventive. She'll never be a diplomat like her father but will turn out OK. So, what's she done?" Ulrika repeated.

"Nothing yet except for being like a third child and causing more worries than my two though my expectations might have been wrong. I was a babysitter throughout childhood and expected that Ingrid would know as much as I do which she didn't. But she picked things up quickly. I now trust her to watch and bathe the kids and they do like her so maybe it's just me," I said.

"Possibly not. Vladimir and I trust your judgment. What happened recently?" Ulrika asked.

"Only what Jenna saw?"

"Which is?"

"The man that Ingrid hung onto. Jenna considers him trouble."

"Have you seen him?" Ulrika asked.

"No, and I explicitly ordered Ingrid not to have a stranger here. I won't risk my family's safety," I replied.

"That's sensible. I would stress it again," Ulrika said.

"Why?"

"For everyone's sake. Ingrid has already had two abortions," Ulrika said.

Chapter 25

"*I'll do that,*" I said slowly, as my brain entered overload.

"I have to go. Beauty is calling. I promised to take her shopping for a new party dress," Ulrika said.

Beauty, her daughter's nickname, *is* beautiful. Early-on, Vladimir began calling her this and it stuck. I envied Ulrika's seemingly placid life even though knowing that it was anything but. The live-in girlfriend of a married, former Russian general who heads an international security company could hardly be that.

My mother and sisters weren't available to babysit so my talk with Ingrid came more quickly than I planned. She looked so sweetly at my dozing babies that my intention faltered until catching myself.

"I must go into the City. I'll be gone until very late and maybe won't return until morning. In an emergency, you have my cell number, my mother's cell number, and the doctor's number. No one but them will enter the house. *Is that clear*?" I said, firmly.

"Crystal," Ingrid replied.

Her cheekiness annoyed me but I remembered what Ulrika said about her and let it pass.

Despite the heavy traffic, I made good time and arrived at Newark Liberty International Airport twenty minutes before Vladimir's plane landed. He was accompanied by an employee, Quincy, a former member of Britain's Special Air Service (SAS). The unit motto is "Who Dares Wins," with which few would disagree.

Vladimir spoke quickly while leading us to the United Club Lounge.

"I have only an hour before the flight to Washington and wanted us to talk," he said.

Then, while snacking on soup and salad in a crowded airport lounge, I told him the decision which was to change my life.

"I want to work with you. I'm not sure it's doable while caring for two babies but am willing to try," I said.

Vladimir rose to hug me tightly and kiss my forehead as Quincy looked away. I had learned during my summer in London that the English aren't comfortable with expressing feelings.

"You'll be given whatever help you need and have authority to decide where the new office is located. Wherever you choose will be fine," he promised.

"Even in Greenwich?" I asked, in a playful yet testing tone.

"If that's what you decide. It wouldn't be a bad choice considering its many wealthy executives and location on the Eastern Corridor. I expect that Ingrid is a big help."

"Yes, she is," I said, but wondered how much he knew.

Chapter 26

I was a long time getting home. Not from dawdling but because a truck/SUV collision had spiraled into a major pileup. The delay gave me time to think.

Despite Vladimir's and Ulrika's confident words, I felt nervous. Managing a security company demanded far more skill than the babysitting service which Erika and I ran during high school. But there is a similarity since client safety is paramount with both, I reassured myself.

I calmed down after remembering my lawyer-father's wise advice: "Don't worry until you have something to worry about." According to the latest radio report, the traffic delay was increasing. The crashed truck had been carrying chemicals which caught fire. Considering its double-lined construction, this was not supposed to happen. Terrorist involvement was believed unlikely but the President had been informed.

I tried phoning home but couldn't get connected. Probably everyone is doing the same, I thought. Traffic finally began moving and I arrived home a little before 1AM, exhausted and needing to pee. After leaving the car in the driveway, I glanced around and froze. An unfamiliar red car was parked in front and the porch light revealed that the front door was ajar.

Though Greenwich's recent rape-murder spree had ended with the criminals' deaths, town residents didn't yet feel safe. Gun sales were still high and most homeowners were armed. I had left my pistol at home since concealed carry permits are issued by states and mine were valid only in Connecticut and New York.

Margaret: Mother of Twins

My 9mm Walther PPS pistol lay in a locked drawer in the library. I quietly retrieved it, instinctively checked that the magazine was full, and unlocked the safety. While climbing the stairs, I heard a cry from above.

Chapter 27

I first checked my children's room. By light from the Disney fixture, I saw them sleeping contentedly. A second cry came from down the hall, in the direction of Ingrid's room. I quietly opened that door and stood stunned, hardly believing my eyes though the happening was obvious even in the low lighting.

Ingrid lay naked on the bed with a man's face between her legs. The cries that I heard were from pleasure and not fear. Her evident enjoyment added to my rage. Wanting to end this scene, I flicked the ceiling light on-and-off. Both froze until the man turned toward me and jumped off the bed. I pointed my pistol at him.

"Move another step and I shoot," I declared, in a no-nonsense tone.

He didn't and Ingrid pleaded, *"Please don't hurt him. I love him."*

"Get dressed, both of you," I ordered, keeping the pistol level.

My fury indicated that there would be no debate.

While they dressed, I gave my final order to the man.

"You are to leave this house and never return, If I see you again, I will knee-cap you and you'll be crippled for life. Do you understand me?"

He didn't reply so I repeated my question and received a sullen "yes."

"Good," I said.

After marching him downstairs, I locked the door and reset the alarm. Then I dealt with Ingrid, feeling greater anger toward her than toward her lover. She had waited in her room.

"How dare you risk the lives of my children by having a stranger in the house. Particularly when I forbade it and they were in your care," I hissed, through gritted teeth.

"I watched them on the video monitor," Ingrid argued.

Realizing that she reasoned like a child, I gave up.

"I want you out of my house. Get packing. You're going home on the next flight to Berlin. I'll pay for your ticket and this month's wages, which is more than you deserve. I won't tell your parents and you can choose what to tell them. You've disappointed me. I believed you more grown-up than you are," I said.

Though still angry, her tears had changed my tone to that of a disenchanted mother.

"Did you give him a key to the house?" I asked.

"Never!"

Whatever her answer, I would have the locks and alarm code changed.

"Get some sleep. You have a big day tomorrow," I said.

Then I went to my children's room, lay on the sofa beside their cribs and slept.

Chapter 28

The next flight to Berlin left from New York City's JFK airport and I had my brother drive Ingrid there. Though having just gotten his license, the City's unforgiving drivers were nothing compared with the peril of his earlier life. And since his girlfriend was drop-dead gorgeous, I could rely on him to ignore Ingrid's wiles.

When they were gone, I phoned the security company and stated what I wanted. They immediately changed the home alarm code and promised to have a locksmith change the locks that day. Only after these were accomplished did I put away my gun.

Then, feeling that Ulrika deserved a heads-up, I phoned her with the news. I hesitated for only a moment, reasoning that Ingrid's risky behavior didn't deserve to be kept confidential.

"I warned you," Ulrika said.

"Yes, you did."

"I've accepted Vladimir's offer," I said.

"He told me and is very pleased. You're a hard worker and will take a load off his shoulders."

"But without Ingrid's help, minimal though it was, I can't be a working mother. I need a live-in assistant, someone to help with the kids, run errands, and act as security in chancy situations. Can you recommend someone?" I asked.

"I get it. You want a heavy with warmth. How soon?" Ulrika asked.

"As soon as possible. I'll initially work from home and will need its security inspected by an expert who can check weekly for wiretaps," I said.

"Those are good ideas. How soon will you look for an office?" Ulrika asked.

"I'll begin when Vladimir tells me my duties," I replied.

"He has a long list," Ulrika said, before hanging up.

Chapter 29

The home inspector who advised the new security scheme was a former Secret Service agent. It included new alarms, geofencing, an interior secret passageway, and enhanced video surveillance using artificial intelligence to alert a command center if someone broke the boundary.

A lingerer at the gate's entrance would receive a tailored warning to leave, stating the color of their clothes. Coming from an unseen speaker, this would scare anyone away. "But the basics are still strong locks and sturdy doors," he said.

While awaiting this installation and Vladimir's orders, my motherhood duties continued. I realized that these would never stop soon after giving birth when I began worrying about my babies all the time though less when my mother babysat.

Nor did I ever stop trying to manage my time better, a task which seemed to become increasingly difficult. My kids had to be fed, bathed, spoken with, and watched continually. What would I do when my roles as mother and executive clashed?

Ingrid's departure was fortunate since her immaturity had added to my worries. But finding a helpful assistant would be difficult since the qualities that I sought don't usually go together. Where could I find a bodyguard who could relate well to babies too? I wondered.

Here, I lucked out. Mila, a bodyguard who worked for Vladimir, had an unusual career. After completing medical school, she was a doctor in Russia's Special Forces before

Vladimir hired her. Now part of Erika's protective detail, she was reassigned to me.

"You couldn't have done me a bigger favor," I gushed, when Vladimir told me of Mila's transfer.

Chapter 30

Mila quickly settled into what had been Ingrid's room. We already knew each other so a getting-to-know-you chat wasn't needed. I told her that, as Vladimir's East Cost manager, I would be handling sensitive matters so her protective duties would be the same as at Erika's home. The only difference would be her occasional watching of my children. If she had other suggestions or needs, I would be open to them.

Mila listened closely. She wasn't disturbed by being older which can make for a touchy relationship. She sensed that I respected her and had molded the job to her strengths. This is how a boss should relate to an employee, Vladimir had advised me.

With this out of the way and cold drinks before us, we settled down for a different kind of talk. An unspoken requirement of her position is that we become close.

"Why do you stay with Vladimir when you could earn three times as much being bodyguard to a billionaire oligarch?" I asked.

"Because he's the smartest person I ever met," Mila said.

"Huh!" burst from me before I could stop it.

"Yes. Despite his age, he believes in technology more than us though differently. He considers it key to keeping our morality in a future that we can barely imagine. Though Russian to the core, he's committed to the American creed that everyone is equal with the individual being the source of authority. This grants them the right to complain about anything, a belief which is still radical in much of the world."

63

Margaret: Mother of Twins

Mila's analysis of Vladimir was what I had long sensed but been unable to express. She and I are on the same wavelength and will be close, I thought.

Chapter 31

My sisters have the irritating habit of showing up unannounced. There is no warning text or phone call, just a ringing of the doorbell. While this behavior is common in Sweden, there's no Scandinavian blood in our ancestry. I get annoyed but not greatly, loving my family too much for that. How will they respond to my new security system's robotic voice? I wondered.

"Are you expecting anyone?" Mila asked.

"No, but my family tends to drop in," I replied.

"I'll get that," she said, and automatically touched to see that her gun was in place.

A small, six-round Kimber Micro pistol firing the 9mm Luger cartridge lay in a rapid-release, outside-the-waistband holster. Her jacket held two extra magazines and a black Kalashnikov switchblade knife with a 3.25" blade. I felt well protected.

Moments later, Mila re-entered the room accompanied by my three sisters bearing packages: a large spinach and feta pie for the adults and, for the children, a Vtech Brilliant Baby Laptop and Tiny Touch Tablet. Both toys were too old for infants but it was a nice gesture. They knew Mila so there was no need for introduction and my explanation was brief.

"Ingrid didn't work out and returned to Germany. Mila will be helping me," I said.

Claudine, my sister and a budding detective, wanted to know more. I avoided replying by asking that she take baby James from my arms. As I expected, this aroused her greater interest. Being an adoptee from drug-addicted parents, she was more grown-up than the typical nine-year-old.

"What's it like being a mother?" she asked.

Answering this required more than momentary thinking.

"It's both the best feeling and the hardest work," I said, finally.

It also wears me out, I thought. But not wanting to confess this, I changed the subject.

"What's happening at home?" I asked.

"Our dad, the Judge, has become a hero!" twenty-three-year-old Melody said proudly.

Chapter 32

My father was always a hero to his kids so it was obvious that Melody meant something different.

"What happened?" I asked.

"Well, he's certainly not a hero to lawyers but he is to the biggest corporations in America. He won't have to worry about getting political contributions," she said.

"I still don't get it," I said, feeling a bit peeved.

Melody had the annoying habit, one which she shared with my boyfriend, Randy, of stringing out stories to increase their suspense.

"What are lawyers famous for?" she asked.

I gave up and answered, realizing that trying to push Melody along wouldn't work. She can be as stubborn as me.

"Hugely inflated fees?" I asked.

"Right. And what would happen to a judge who tried to stop this?"

"He'd get hordes of lawyers trying to end his career but move onto the fast track into Heaven."

"And?"

"Become the darling of corporations who would happily bankroll his re-election campaign," I said.

Melody thrust that morning's issue of *The Wall Street Journal* into my face. A bold headline read, "Gutsy Judge Battles Lawyer Fee Corruption." The article began, "Lawyers tend to set arbitrary fees which have little to do with their work, feeling that their clients are easily intimidated or, with corporations, too rich to object. But with changes to the economy and technology, companies have begun to care."

"I didn't know that dad cared so much about corporations," I said.

"He doesn't but the lawyers' demands were outrageous. Dad's ruling opened state investigations across America."

Melody was working in a local attorney's office until beginning law school. A movie lover since childhood, her interest had been entertainment law but her enthusiasm caused me to wonder if her focus was changing.

I read aloud from the article: "According to the legal ruling, the law firm billed the company for fifty-hour workdays, the cost of heating and air-conditioning their offices, commuting between homes and offices, thirty-thousand-dollars for ground transportation during a two-week trial in Chicago, and eleven hours of work for three letters that were two sentences each."

Feeling stunned by such arrogance, I looked at the others. Even Mila was awestruck.

"Such conceit and contempt," she said.

I couldn't describe it better.

Chapter 33

We noshed and gossiped comfortably until Melody raised the issue which I had been trying to forget.

"How is your support group going?" she asked.

Not wanting to reply, I pointed to a fragment of food on her mouth. Ignoring my rudeness, she wiped it away and repeated the question.

"I'm beginning to be sorry that I started it. It's evolving in odd ways," I said.

"How?" Melody persisted.

Explaining presented a problem since the group had a moral expectation of confidentiality. We met to help each other, not gain titillating gossip to share with friends. But telling a little would be acceptable, I quickly decided.

"My motive for starting the group was needing help. A support group helped Hillary after the murder of her mother, sharing with others who experienced the same. I thought that a group might help my move from being a student to the working mother of twins," I said.

"That would drive anyone crazy!" asserted Claudine, with her often adult sophistication.

I made a rueful smile and continued.

"The others' problems aren't common like mine. One woman can't leave her married gangster lover and another fears that her roommate is a terrorist," I said.

The ensuing silence was broken by Mila.

"As the group leader, what are you supposed to do?" she asked, rhetorically.

"Exactly," I said.

"You're a godsend!" Melody said, abruptly.

"I don't view it that way," I said.

"Because you're not seeing it clearly. You manage the office of a security company. Who better could they hope for?" Melody asked.

When considering this, I realized that she was right.

Chapter 34

My twins awoke, first Donna and then James. They were hungry and I did my duty, unembarrassed since no men were around. Melanie's interest in the process didn't please me. A second teenage mother is certainly not what my parents want, I thought. While the nursing calmed me, I still needed help and turned toward the others.

"What can I do?" I asked.

Mila answered first, being experienced as a doctor, soldier, and bodyguard to the rich and famous.

"Concentrate on one person's problem at a time and a solution may present itself. Each will view it differently though that might not help," she said.

"Why not?" I asked.

"Because nothing will change if a person isn't ready to hear what's needed or can't do it," Melody exclaimed.

"Yes," I agreed.

"It may not be as hard as you think. The big problem of the woman with the Mafia boyfriend is psychological. He's likely had many girlfriends so the glue bonding them is her's. Powerful lovers are intoxicating. They get rapid service in restaurants and elsewhere. People give in from fear. Who would freely exchange this for an everyday life?" Mila asked, rhetorically.

"He can walk away but she can't," I summarized.

"Not without support," Mila said.

"She has her therapist," I argued.

Margaret: Mother of Twins

"Joining your group shows that she needs more," Mila said, firmly.

I couldn't argue with her logic.

Chapter 35

"I don't see what I can add since my life has been so different from theirs," I argued.

I felt myself drawing away as my mind returned to my babies.

"Sometimes, people just need a caring friend to listen," Claudine said.

Once again, the adult insight of her nine-year-old mind astonished me. Or are you so worn out that you can't think clearly, I asked myself.

"How much talking did your therapist do?" Melody asked.

"Ten-percent of the time," I replied.

"That proves Claudine's point," Melody said.

They're ganging up against me, I thought.

"Enough! I get it," I said, in a bitchy tone.

Only the babies' murmurs broke the ensuing silence. I handed Donna to Melanie, leaned back on the sofa and closed my eyes until my phone's vibration jarred me upright.

"Can I come over?" Randy asked.

"You're always welcome, by me and your children," I said, warmly.

"See you, love," he said, and hung up.

"Randy is coming," I told the others.

Then, not wanting our get-together to be mostly my complaining, I turned toward Melody.

"How are things with your boyfriend's lawsuit?" I asked.

While a newly licensed physician, Jack had the bad luck to be drawn into the lawsuit against the practice where he worked. He was in the room when the patient was being treated by a senior doctor and never even spoke to her. Our father had advised Jack about court procedure to reduce his stress. Being sued can drive people crazy.

Melody told this to Mila before bringing the rest of us up-to-date.

"The doctor gave his insurance company permission for a settlement conference. If the patient accepts the amount, it'll be over next week."

"So, are you two engaged?" Melanie asked, maintaining her reputation for asking unwelcome questions.

"*Maybe*," Melody replied, with a smile.

"Just maybe?" Melanie persisted.

Melody didn't answer and her smile hardened. Randy's arrival can't be too soon, I thought.

Chapter 36

No more was said about Melody's boyfriend after Randy arrived. Randy liked Jack but had the usual male disinterest in engagements. Though now a father, he wasn't yet a family man.

Randy would play endlessly any child and they loved him. But their lives were another's responsibility. They could be left without feeling guilty. I hoped for him to outgrow this immaturity before our children were much older.

With this in mind, I handed James to Randy as soon as he arrived. Randy self-consciously took him, and James smiled in response to Randy's baby talk.

I placed our daughter beside them and indicated the kitchen for the rest of us. With the doors open, I could hear if there was a problem. I wanted Randy to be alone with his children. On some future day I would send him on their playdate.

As my sisters left, a Special Delivery envelope arrived from Vladimir. He has sent me work, I instantly thought, and was correct.

Vladimir's message described the structure of the business, its key officers, and the services that the company marketed for individuals and governments.

I was instructed to hire an assistant and rent an office. Long before, I had been given a corporate credit card to use for business expenses.

A copy of a corporate resolution, with seal affixed, was enclosed. It was open-ended and permitted me to hire employees, rent office space, open bank accounts, or whatever else was needed. The document reflected trust and I felt humble.

Even before receiving it, I realized that I needed more help since family members wouldn't always be available to babysit. But where might I find her?

"At the high school?" Mila suggested.

That sounded good to me.

Chapter 37

Walking through Greenwich High School felt strange. The building seemed smaller than when I attended, as usually happens when an adult returns to their childhood place.

The Principal listened thoughtfully as I described my need for an on-call babysitter. I would pay twenty-five dollars an hour including for travel time to and from their home. There would be a five-hundred-dollar bonus after a year's satisfactory service. These terms were generous but, as Erika said, paying well insures against lousy work. "Usually," she then added.

The Principal promised to get back to me, saying that he knew of a smart student who might be perfect. She was in her Junior year and her family was poor. The Principal remembered me and our meeting was cordial despite my dual objectionable status as a single mother/college dropout.

My last trip that day was to the phone company, to order my home's internet speed increased and three more phone lines, one for faxing. I would have a home-office like my lawyer-father.

While driving home, I considered where to locate the official office. My choices were few unless I wanted to move. Manhattan is a prized business location but would require an unappealing commute. White Plains, in nearby New York State, was closer but less prestigious. An impressive office overlooking Greenwich Harbor would do.

I decided this while parking at home. Then, satisfied with the day's accomplishments, I relaxed with my babies until their bedtime. Then, Randy would put us all to bed.

Chapter 38

"It's not like before..." Randy said.

"No," I said, simply.

He didn't need to explain. Despite completing my day's tasks, I couldn't relax and our sex showed it. Instead of relating to our bodies, my mind remained on our infants though they slept well.

Thoughts about Randy's erection problem poured through me. In the past he had blamed it on worry about an exam. Now, he had no exams so was the cause my changed body? Was my looser vagina less appealing? He had loved how tight it was before I gave birth. Or was it my being a mother and not simply the girlfriend, or the randy whore that some men fantasize?

"I'm sorry," Randy said.

"Don't. We're human, not machines. I'm tense and maybe your body reacted to it," I said, supportively.

Another woman might then have suggested a drink or cigarette but there were none in this Mormon household. I offered what I consider better.

"Want some cocoa?" I asked.

"To use how..." Randy teased.

With this playfulness, I knew that he was OK.

I went downstairs while he checked on the babies. This wasn't needed since an audio-video feed of them was in my bedroom. But I was glad since it showed that Randy was becoming a family man.

After my return, we talked like an ordinary married couple.

"Have you rented an office yet?" Randy asked.

"Tomorrow. It'll probably be in one of the new buildings along the waterfront," I said.

Randy nodded agreement. He attended Yale in New Haven and were my office in Manhattan we would hardly see each other.

"Is anything else new?" he asked.

"I'll be interviewing a high school girl as an on-call babysitter and am fixing up a home-office. I'll only go to the official one for meetings," I said.

"That'll made things easier," Randy said.

I nodded and we finished our cocoa in silence.

After turning out the light, he reached for me. Our problem with sex had disappeared.

Chapter 39

I didn't entirely trust my judgment in hiring. While running our babysitter referral service during high school, Erika and I had always hired together, believing that our intuitions would balance. This proved true and our business thrived. For this reason I asked Erika to interview my prospective babysitter with me.

Apart from the information provided by her school principal, I knew nothing about Maria. She was sixteen, smart, headed the school's math team, and came from a poor family. No teacher had ever complained about her which is more than can be said about me though I did avoid anything serious.

I scheduled the interview at my home. It would be vital to see how Maria interacted with James and Donna. The rest would be icing on the cake.

"She's prompt," Erika remarked, as Maria's voice came through the speaker at the gate.

Promptness is a Godly virtue for irreligious Erika. Another is frugality. This may seem odd for a billionaire's daughter but, as I've said before, their lives are not like your's and mine.

Maria was tall and almost anorexically thin. Her straight black hair was worn long, half-way down her back. She wore too formal clothes for a teenager and I wondered if they were a relative's. I knew from personal experience how poor children must dress.

After meeting her at the door, I invited her into the living room where Erika sat with the children. She refused my offer of water or juice and the interview began.

Margaret: Mother of Twins

"The Principal recommended you highly," I said.

"He's kind," Maria said.

I noted her poise and good self-control.

"Let me tell you something about my family," I began. "I was a student at Barnard College until becoming pregnant. I'm the mother of twins and help manage my father's security business. I'm setting up a home office here and will be leasing an official office on the waterfront.

"I need a reliable babysitter to work on-call. This will be on evenings or weekends, outside of your school hours. You'll never be alone here. Because of the nature of the business, I have a live-in bodyguard, Mila.

"The pay is twenty-five dollars an hour, including for travel time to and from your home. You're guaranteed ten hours a week whether or not you're needed. There is a five-hundred-dollar bonus after a year's satisfactory service. Does this interest you?" I asked.

In response, Maria began crying.

Chapter 40

"I'm sorry," Maria said.

"There's no need. I've done the same," I said quickly.

"But not on a job interview."

"No, but I haven't had to go on any," I said.

"I need the job."

"Can you stay for brunch with us and the kids?" I asked.

I wanted this for two reasons: to see how well she related to them, and to learn about her family. Was her marked slimness psychologically caused or did it result from her family's poverty? I wondered.

I set a simple meal of bagels, cheeses, and left-over cold baked salmon from the previous day's dinner. Maria ate hungrily as I learned her story.

She had a six-year-old brother, Jacob. Her mother had made the common mistake of choosing a spouse based on looks and not character, though he was smart enough to earn a six-figure income as a computer systems manager. Soon after her brother was born, their father relocated to Singapore and hadn't been heard from since. Nor did he pay child-support.

Maria's mother supported the family with her earnings as a cleaning woman. This had been OK since there were always Greenwich families seeking good service. But the internet changed this industry. No longer were domestic workers sought through word-of-mouth praise. Instead, they were hired via an app which promised pre-screened help at lower cost. Her mother, a computer-illiterate, couldn't compete and the family fell on hard times. Did Maria starve herself so her mother and brother could eat? I wondered.

"What kind of work do you see yourself doing when you're older?" Erika asked.

I sensed that her question reflected more than curiosity.

"Something involving math and programming. I'm taking Advanced Placement classes in both and got good scores on the PSAT: a perfect 760 on the Math though only a 740 on the Reading and Writing. Maybe good enough to earn a college scholarship somewhere," Maria said, hesitantly.

"Those are wonderful scores!" I blurted, forgetting my role as prospective employer.

Erika was equally impressed. Her scores had totaled 1470 and mine were lower: Perfect on the Reading and Writing but only 650 on the Math. I hadn't expected to do better. Randy is the mathematician in my family.

"My dad's companies are always looking for talented interns. Some are given a scholarship, and a job offer after graduation. I'll tell him about you," Erika said.

Now, Maria didn't cry but her eyes shone with tears.

Chapter 41

"I've been babysitting my brother forever," Maria said.

I smiled and nodded supportively. She related to James and Donna as well as any babysitter that I'd known. They babbled baby talk and she babbled baby talk and all got on swimmingly. After learning this, I ended the interview.

I later learned that Maria's thinness resulted from unhappiness. Her first love affair, with Barton, had ended badly two months earlier.

Being two years older and more experienced, Barton had easily seduced her with such endearments as buying her chocolates when she had her period. I was given barely a kiss after giving birth. Randy needs educating, I told myself. Just before Maria left, I spoke with Erika alone in the kitchen.

"Maria seems OK," she said.

"Yes, but I'll have Vladimir check out her family. One can't be too careful," I said.

"You're right. She rode her bike over. I'll drive her home and maybe get more information. What are you doing this afternoon?" Erika asked.

"My mom's free to babysit so I thought I'd look for an office. Want to come?"

Erika is a far better negotiator than me and I was glad that she did. She would prevent me from being screwed. I was a manager-in-training and every decision that I made would be carefully examined. Leasing an office was new for me and even scarier than giving birth.

"How big a space will you need?" Erika asked in the car.

"Four rooms: a small reception room; a room to hold files and office equipment; one room as office and a larger one for conferences. In a building with a view, ideally of the waterfront, and within walking distance of the train station," I said.

"That sounds right. Let's get started," Erika said.

We did.

Chapter 42

The office that I leased wasn't my ideal but would do. Fantasies rarely come true. It was in a new six-story building, close by the railroad station and thus convenient for travelers from Manhattan.

After the killing of Greenwich's serial rapist months before, the town had resumed its casual attitude toward safety. But I am innately cautious. The building's reception desk boasted a retired police officer to check visitors and all corridors had video surveillance.

"We take security seriously since some hedge fund employees work past midnight. The building is always open and there is only one entrance. At night, a guard accompanies each tenant to their car," the manager informed us.

"What's not to like?" Erika said, approvingly, once we were alone.

I signed a five-year lease with the option to renew for an additional ten-years. Erika negotiated the yearly rent increase down from the manager's demand of ten-percent to one-percent.

"That's what he expected. Only an idiot would pay ten-percent and he knew it!" Erika said.

This shows why I wanted her with me.

On the way home, we stopped at a local furniture store for desks, sofas, chairs, and filing cabinets. Their delivery was promised the next day. I returned home with a sense of achievement, feeling ready for whatever duties came my way.

My mother had something else on her mind.

"Have you thought about getting married?" she asked, as my children dozed.

I chewed slowly on one of my mother's addictive chocolate/peanut butter cookies to give myself time to think.

"Randy isn't ready," I said, finally.

It's hard for a single mother not to feel defensive when asked about marrying the father of her children. I credited not being given a hard time to the parenting group that my mother attended at our local Mormon Church. Still, her question hurt.

"When I want something and your father doesn't, I let him think he's right. This plants a seed in his mind so when he thinks about it again, he believes that it's *his* idea and does what I want," my mother advised.

Her advice shocked me and it showed.

"This is why you still need your mother," she said, with a smile.

Chapter 43

I returned to my most important job of being a mother. Even at two months of age, I saw personality differences between James and Donna. He was more active and she was more thoughtful. Did this observation reflect my belief in the basic differences between boys and girls or is it true? I asked myself. I enjoyed babbling with and musing about them until Jenna called.

"Have you thought more about the group?" she asked.

I hadn't but didn't want to say.

"A little. How about you?" I asked.

"Sam's problem seems most important. We should work on it first," Jenna said.

"Sam?"

That I couldn't remember who she is showed how out-of-it I felt.

"*Samantha*. The woman who's afraid that her landlord is a terrorist. You remember!"

Now I did.

"Of course," I lied. "Maybe you should raise the issue. How are things going?"

"Better. I'm off all meds and help my dad do paperwork. I really am better," she insisted.

After her rescue from being sex trafficked, Jenna was prescribed medication to reduce her anxiety and help her sleep. She had isolated herself until being coaxed by Erika's father who had become Jenna's step-father. Unlike some merged families, theirs blended well.

"Come over. It's time for my babies to meet their new aunt," I pleaded.

While strictly not an aunt, Jenna was caring and the meeting would be good for all.

I understood the silence before Jenna replied. Being raped had made her feel dirty, even inhuman. Should someone like me be allowed near children? she was probably asking herself.

"I will, and bring presents too," Jenna said, finally.

"Your presence will be their best gift," I said, and meant it.

Chapter 44

Playing with young kids perked up Jenna, as can happen with anyone. Meanwhile, I attended to my next task: hiring an assistant.

Whether male or female wouldn't matter but being honest and reliable did. Where could I find such a person? Not yet having gained a business network, I powered up my laptop, signed onto the biggest hiring site, and wrote an ad. As words flowed, the characteristics of who I sought became clearer.

Being a security company, I preferred someone with a police or military background. They must be personable since they would be meeting wealthy clients and government officials. They would have to be capable of making decisions independently since, when responsible for others' safety, one can't predict what might arise.

With these characteristics in mind, I posted the following somewhat vague ad: "The manager of an international security company located in Greenwich, Connecticut seeks an assistant, preferably with a military or police background. Duties are varied and include seeking clients and writing reports. Pay and benefits are excellent and include relocation expenses. Fingerprinting, drug-testing, and background investigation will be conducted before hiring. E-mail resume, contact information of two references and signed consent for them to provide information to the company. Interview expenses will be paid."

"I can't improve on that," Erika said, when she read it before my posting.

"How about interviewing candidates with me?" I asked.

"Using FaceTime?" Erika asked.

"No. Some things can only be sensed in person and FaceTime only works on Apple, not Windows," I said.

"You could use Skype," Erika said.

"I want to see them in person," I repeated.

"Like you can't smell a blind date over the phone," Erika said, with a smile.

"Exactly," I said, and smiled too.

"This reminds me of when we hired babysitters together," Erika said.

"That was another life," I said, with a sigh.

James' cry, soon joined by Donna's, confirmed this.

Chapter 45

Few of the thirty-nine replies to the ad kept my attention. Those with grammatical or spelling errors were a no-starter for me. The rest were unsuitable, like from one who seemed a failed insurance salesman.

I finally did what I should have done originally: contact the non-profit organization which sought employment for newly-discharged military. The day after faxing them my needs, I received a phone call from its director.

"Your job sounds great!" she gushed.

"For the right person," I cautioned.

"Of course, but we don't run a meat market. I'll send you *one* resume. Passing a drug test and getting references won't be a problem."

This was how I found my assistant. After graduating from West Point, Jordan served the obligatory five-years before leaving the Army. His marriage was solid but his wife couldn't tolerate the confines of military life. She was pregnant and wanted him present during delivery, which no soldier could promise. After Jordan left, I mused with Erika about the interview.

"You won't get better. He's presentable, smart, educated about security, and not so much older than you that the age difference would matter. And having a pregnant wife makes him ready to settle down. What pay will you offer?" Erika asked.

"More than he got in the military. Ninety-five-thousand a year with a two-thousand a month housing subsidy to make up for our higher living cost than at his last post in North Carolina," I said.

"Plus a leased car?" Erika asked.

"If nothing else persuades him, the BMW should," I said.

"And an SUV for his wife too?" Erika asked, with a small smile.

"A boss must be tough to be respected. I'm not *that* generous with the company's money," I said.

Chapter 46

Jordan's wife, Elizabeth, accompanied him to Greenwich for their inspection visit. They got the grand tour or what substitutes for it here.

Erika's bodyguard, black-suited Abram, drove us around in the imposing, armored SUV. After passing several large estates, they were shown the North Street Elementary School and Greenwich High School. I mentioned that their student-teacher ratio of thirteen is probably the lowest in America.

We then toured the Greenwich Library, scanned its lengthy list of children's activities, and stopped for a snack in its downstairs café.

Erika pointed out her favorite stores during our stroll down Greenwich Avenue. We lunched at L'Escale, an upscale French restaurant with a splendid water view. There, I described our company.

"Our home office is in Berlin with a secondary office in London. Greenwich has been chosen for its East Coast office. We provide security for corporate executives and wealthy individuals, and special services for governments," I began.

Jordan seemed upset at my mention of "special services" so I described them.

"These are para-military and *always* have government approval, as our recent rescue of sex-trafficked women in Europe. You won't be involved with this. They're all former Special Forces soldiers from America and Europe. Most are Russian, as is our principal director, Vladimir, who is a retired general," I said.

I felt it best to get this fact out of the way and was right. Both Jordan and Elizabeth looked startled, as if their previously enjoyable tour had led to my invitation to join a spy ring. I couldn't help smiling.

"We're not what you might think. Vladimir is my father and his fellow directors are retired from Britain's Secret Intelligence Service and the Central Intelligence Agency. The company is divorced from politics and contracts only with Western nations. We're legitimate with high ethics. If our proposal meets your needs, you'll meet Vladimir before making your decision," I said.

After describing the salary and benefits, I awaited their acceptance. Jordan would not find better.

Chapter 47

"That's more than I've been offered and the benefits are extraordinary," Jordan said.

"We hire for the long-term. We want our job to be your last until you retire, *if* you choose to retire. My father is going strong in his sixties. I was chosen as his replacement but he now says that he can't afford to retire since my baby step-sister was born," I said.

"What's he like?" Elizabeth asked.

"As a person or a boss?" I asked, with a smile.

"Both."

I thought for a moment before answering.

"He's had a strange life, having survived Communism and resettlement in the West. He was a general in Russia's Presidential Security Service and fought in Afghanistan earlier. The business began small with retired soldiers protecting wealthy tourists in Russia. It is now international with our para-military unit being added a decade ago.

"*Fire Storm* does mostly hostage rescue. Rescuing the sex-trafficked women gained us good publicity and more government contracts. American, British, German, and Russian intelligence services aided in that rescue."

We exchanged smiles at the end of the lunch. I said that I needed his decision quickly and he promised an answer within a day. Elizabeth's glowing eyes told me what it would be.

"That's three down. You've hired a babysitter, rented an office, and almost certainly hired a good-looking assistant," Erika said, with a small smile.

"Damn, but he's married too," I said, playfully, before becoming serious. "It's the group's problems that worry me," I said."

"It's giving you more work than support. Why not end it?" Erika asked.

"I can't. It would be like reading a thriller and never learning how things worked out," I said.

Chapter 48

I created the group to feel less depressed but it was having the opposite effect. Still, our Manhattan meetings became an excuse for Erika to do more of her "serious shopping." She was bright-eyed and sunny that day, a mood which I hesitated to change with my gloomy thoughts. So I simply listened as she shared the happy events of her now settled life.

"I feel guilty being close to Sara. It's as if I'm damaging my mother's memory," Erika said.

Erika's mother was murdered a decade before and Sara was her step-mother. With her father's re-marriage, Erika also gained a step-brother and two step-sisters. Unlike many blended families, her's resembled those of heartening TV series. I envied her calm, which is rarely experienced by mothers of multiples.

"You won't have to do anything," she coaxed supportively. "I'll set out the food and you can vent and relax. It'll all work out. Sam's 'terrorist roommate' will turn out to be a traveling movie producer. Vera and Joanne and Krystal will find loving husbands, and Enid will lose her married Mafia lover," Erika cheerfully predicted.

"He'll die in a shoot-out?" I said, not buying her optimism.

"Well, that *would* end her fear of leaving."

"Not if he became her lover-ideal, never to be found again. Then her love life would be over since no living person can compete with a ghost. Rational thought is easily lost inside the emotional baggage of guilt," I said.

Margaret: Mother of Twins

But Erika was having none of my gloom. Becoming silent, she spoke again only as our car entered The Dakota's driveway.

"I ordered your favorite: baked salmon and German rye bread. You'll feel better," she predicted.

I hoped.

Chapter 49

All but Krystal arrived promptly. She phoned a few minutes later, stating that she couldn't make this meeting. A client with an emergency had showed up unexpectedly. She promised to come the following week and I readily understood. Before becoming a judge, my father often came home late from his law practice.

The table was lain with sliced turkey, salmon, Swiss and Muenster cheese, bread, bagels, mini-bottles of water and juice, and a carafe of coffee. My horseradish mustard hadn't been forgotten. Once I started eating, I did feel better. Conversation was subdued with small talk until I spoke.

"It might be best to focus on one issue at a time. Since Sam's problem seems immediate, would anyone object if we began with it?" I asked.

No one did. Sam hadn't stopped eating when I spoke and I wondered if she normally ate enough. Youth eating habits often aren't good. She finished chewing and looked up from her plate.

"What I said about my landlord, Anna, *is* weird when you come down to it. Maybe she likes to travel, like a doctor who works part-time in different states or something equally ordinary," Sam said.

"But you sense things about her that don't fit. That's how I learned about my boyfriend. He early-on told me that he was married but not that he'd been arrested," Enid said.

"Arrested?" Joanne asked, having apparently forgotten Enid's story.

"He's involved with organized crime, formerly called the Mafia. Their activity peaked decades ago. So what did you sense?" Enid asked.

"Something I'd have a hard time explaining. Call it my instinct that she's faking being normal," Sam said.

"We all play roles, behave differently with different people," I objected.

Sam began munching on a slice of Swiss cheese. The rest of us remained silent, recognizing that she needed time to think. Finally, she spoke.

"When Anna smiles, her eyes are hooded like a cobra's," Sam said.

Chapter 50

The word "cobra" stopped conversation. We stared at Sam until, believing that it was the leader's role to act, I risked my question, feeling that she *must* have noticed more even if being unaware of it.

"What else about Anna seems strange?" I asked.

This silence grew so long that Jenna and Enid resumed eating and I did too.

"She's *too* interested in my friends going to grad school, particularly those in the sciences. She offered to hold a party for them and cater it. Why would an older woman so greatly want to meet students that she'd pay for it? It doesn't make sense," Sam said.

"It would be a cheap way to recruit them," I said.

My twin brother had been recruited as a sleeper agent before his rescue.

"For what?" Enid asked.

"A science student who is an American citizen could be valuable after graduating. Consider their spying opportunities in industry and government for a foreign nation," I said.

My statement shocked the group into silence, as had Sam's use of the word "cobra."

"What would make Anna stand out personally?" I asked.

"The lipstick she wears?" Sam asked.

"If it's relevant," I replied, feeling annoyed.

"No, I'm jumpy and being silly. Anna *is* odd but in ordinary ways. She has a knack for putting people at ease. She'll sing along with Amazon Music but with more passion than ability.

"At first, her quickness to express emotion made me feel she's honest. Like when the building's super needed a part and couldn't make a quick repair, she cursed but immediately apologized and gave him a twenty-dollar tip. She's very likable," Sam said.

"She might be a perfect agent, especially since her appearance is so ordinary that you haven't said a word about it," I said.

Chapter 51

Being the group leader and feeling that we were missing a devil's advocate, I presented that argument.

"Let's summarize what Sam told us. Anna is congenial but has a nasty streak, has forgettable looks, and likes to be with young people. Wouldn't that describe me?" I asked, with a smile.

"Your looks aren't ordinary," Jenna objected.

"Only on my best days," I said, modestly.

Vera turned toward Sam.

"Meg is right. Of all the possibilities, what makes you fear that your landlord is a terrorist?" Vera asked.

I said nothing though hating to be called "Meg." A group leader must be accepting, I reminded myself.

"I don't know. Maybe because there are so many police on the subway and warnings to report suspicious behavior," Sam admitted.

"You want our advice about whether to report her," I suggested.

"I guess that's about it," Sam said.

"Don't knock yourself. Telling us was smart since you have a good deal on the apartment. Causing trouble would risk losing it and you wouldn't want that. Can I change the subject?" Jenna said, turning toward me.

"I'm not the boss. We're all equal here. It might be good to deal with another issue until Sam gets more information," I said.

"Do it carefully!" I warned Sam, in a serious tone and looking directly at her.

"Carefully!" she repeated, with a small smile.

I immediately felt nervous. *Would* Sam be cautious? I had smiled like that with my mother when I was about to do something risky. But Sam is an adult, I told myself.

All eyes turned toward Jenna, who seemed to have a hard time speaking. When she did, her tone was both hesitant and pleading.

"A guy wants to date me, a software programmer I met in Starbucks. He's thirty, with two children. His wife lost custody after being arrested for dealing drugs. How can I tell him I was a whore? But knowing that, would he want me around his kids?" she asked.

Chapter 52

"Being raped once is bad enough but I was raped hundreds of times. This was after being beaten with electrical wires and burned on the arm with cigarettes while being *broken in.* I had become the property of the pimp who bought me. Some girls felt so hopeless that they killed themselves after being forced to service a dozen men a day," Jenna said.

Her matter-of-fact tone disturbed us more than her words.

"How did you survive?" Enid asked, slowly.

Living with a criminal, she might be asking herself the same question, I thought, but didn't say.

"By tuning out and feeling nothing. When recovering from surgery as a kid, the doctor didn't want to prescribe an opioid to reduce pain and taught me self-hypnosis. I used it when the hurt got too great. The anal sex made me feel that I was being torn in two," she said.

Enough, I thought. *More,* and the group will end which I now didn't want.

"You've survived pain and witnessed death, experiencing the near-equivalent of a concentration camp. Why do you feel so unworthy that you shouldn't associate with children, who are as innocent as you were? You must say *yes* to life by forcing yourself to be active. Turn your suffering into accomplishment by discarding your needless guilt," Joanne advised.

These words seemed to resonate with Jenna, perhaps because of Joanne's suffering as a widow with three young children. Being the oldest of us, her maturity gave the perspective which we lacked.

A calming silence descended after Joanne spoke. May I become equally wise, I hoped.

Chapter 53

The meeting left me emotionally drained. I was glad when it was over and the others seemed to feel the same. We hugged each other and left quickly. Only when the car left The Dakota's driveway did I speak.

"Thank you for your honesty," I said, to Jenna.

"It's a good group. I feel better," she said.

Despite the horror that she revealed, Jenna looked serene. I leaned into the cushions and closed my eyes. A hand clasped mine and I opened them.

"You did good," Erika said.

We are as close as sisters and there was no need to reply. I again closed my eyes and in a minute was asleep.

Though missing my babies, they didn't seem to miss me. They were having a joyful time with my mother and youngest sister when I arrived, talking baby-talk and playing with the new toys of that morning.

More such presents and I'll need a bigger house, I told myself, blaming this bitchiness on feeling guilty for having left James and Donna for even those few hours. When I confided this to my mother, she gently remarked, "It's a frequent mother thing."

"How did your group go?" she asked.

"Very well! Jenna told her story, Joanne, the widow with three kids, gave advice, and everyone was moved. I had been uneasy about starting the group but no longer," I said.

"You need something cheerful and I have just the thing," my mother said.

I looked at her hopefully as she handed me a thick envelope.

"This was addressed to you at our house: Grandma Stella arrives tomorrow to visit," she said.

"But she lives in Utah," I said, stupidly.

"Yes, and airlines fly from there to here."

"I'm sorry. I'm worn out," I said, apologetically.

My mother smiled.

"That's another mother thing," she said.

Chapter 54

Grandma Stella's letter was short on words and filled with photos. I had many relatives in Utah and knew none. They were tall and short and mostly blond with wide smiles.

The Eastern and Western branches of our family have little contact except for holiday cards. The reason seems to derive from an ancient feud which no one talks about or maybe even knows.

Or it might simply be our different lives and beliefs. We are all Mormon but those in Utah are passionate about it. Had we lived there, neither Randy nor Erika would be welcome in my family for both aren't religious, Erika's family celebrates Christmas at the latest celebrated restaurant.

Among Stella's photos was one of the church they attended. Nestled under large oak trees, I learned that an ancestor had been a carpenter who helped construct it and the adjoining parsonage in 1893. In its cornerstone was a gold piece, an ear of corn, and a Bible. These indicated that if anything bad happened, the congregation would be strong enough to overcome it. "But the church stands as strong and tall as when it was built," the letter read.

This devotion seemed familiar, as would that for members of any religion many generations later. Like a Jewish ceremony today would be to Moses.

Some pictures made me curious what Stella thought of us: her photos of a railroad station, children wading in mud puddles, and families on horseback.

"Why did she send these?" I asked.

"She obviously doesn't know your opinion about horseback riding," my mother replied.

I was on a horse only once, at an indoor riding stable when I was six. Sitting high-up on the huge animal terrified me and I would never ride again.

"Stella means well," my mother said.

"So did the horse," I said.

I still felt anger at that gentle creature. Irrational feelings have a way of lingering.

Chapter 55

Stella looked the archetype of a grandmother. Nearer eighty than seventy, she was tall, gray-haired and plump. But her eyes were clear and so was her mind. Though fearing Grandma Stella's criticisms, her visit turned out to be a welcome relief. She loved my house, which was inherited from another grandmother, and promised to send ancestral furnishings.

She said nothing about my unmarried motherhood, which is frowned on by Mormons, and praised my children's beauty.

When she did ask about their father, I said that he studied computer science at Yale and planned to get a doctorate. Computer companies are big in Utah and this impressed her. "Like Bill Gates," she said, admiringly. While Randy *is* smart, his being a good father is more important to me.

Stella told me that my Cousin Rachel had left her corporate job for a mountain homestead to raise sheep, dairy goats, and working horses. She also made soap, knitted, and taught classes on how to raise chickens. It was implied that I should follow in her footsteps but I felt exhausted enough.

Noting this, she hugged us again and, before leaving, vowed that *all* my Utah relatives would soon visit their newest. I managed a smile. Stella was staying with my mother and I phoned her an hour later.

"What did Stella think?" I asked.

"She gave you her biggest compliment," my mother said.

"Which is?"

"That you and Randy and James and Donna belong in Utah," my mother replied.

Chapter 56

Things were calmer the rest of the week. Until hearing from Vladimir, my only duty was being a mother. James and Donna seemed to appreciate this too.

Wanting to be present when the office furniture was delivered, I scheduled this when both my mother and the new babysitter could babysit. While I still believed that hiring Maria was a good decision, my innate caution wanted my mother to check her out too. There's a difference between being paranoid and being sensibly watchful.

The delivery men arrived on time and arranged the furniture as I instructed. The phone and internet hookups had already been made and I checked to see that they worked.

These chores hadn't taken long. Drunk with freedom, I stopped downtown and wandered into the opening at a gallery which specialized in early 20th century European art. Erika had bought one of their paintings as a present for her father and his bride. It seemed an odd wedding gift but, I reminded myself, members of billionaire families don't do the ordinary

Needing to pee, I went to the large well-furnished bathroom. There, leaning against a washstand, I found a woman breastfeeding.

"Many bathrooms are filthy but this one is spotless. I couldn't find another place to be alone. No one else had a young child and I was getting weird stares," she said.

I said that I had two infants and understood.

"I usually do business reporting for *The Wall Street Journal* but our arts reporter is out sick. This was a rush assignment and I couldn't get a babysitter. Liz is four-months-old and if I'm not with her, I have to pump every few hours. Businesses don't make it easy for working mothers. They should have lactation rooms just like they have bathrooms. Shouldn't women be asked what they want?" she asked, rhetorically.

"I couldn't agree more!" I said.

Her rushed tone showed the anxiety common to the mothers of infants and we instantly bonded, exchanging business cards before parting.

Friendship with a business reporter is an asset to every corporate manager. You're behaving like an executive, I told myself, with satisfaction.

Chapter 57

My kids were asleep when I arrived home. Maria was upset but I didn't learn this until later.

"She's wonderful with the babies but unhappy," my mother confided.

"What's wrong?" I asked, nervously.

"The usual for her age: boy trouble," my mother replied.

"She told me about it," I said.

"But she's good with James and Donna!" my mother insisted.

She likes her, I thought.

"Was the office furniture delivered?" my mother asked.

"It went fine. There's no more to do and I can stay home for a while."

"Don't be a stranger!" my mother politely demanded before leaving.

My becoming a mother had sent both our lives onto unfamiliar paths, I thought. I resumed my routine: caring for my babies and the house, rearranging furniture, and keeping Randy up to date while fantasizing our future.

He had been taking nearly a double course load and would graduate from Yale early. Graduate school beckoned and, considering his talent, his admission to the best of them was certain but so were his responsibilities.

Margaret: Mother of Twins

Randy now had permanent legal obligations, James and Donna, and one non-legal one, me. While I felt sure of his commitment, career is foremost in the minds of young men. If an unbeatable offer came from Stanford or CalTech, would he jump ship? Follow the old American saying to "Go West, young man." I didn't think so but this worry persisted.

Vladimir phoned. He praised my hiring of Jordan, adding that this evidenced his faith in my management ability. He considered it best that Jordan do the travel and sales calls until my children were older. My next assignment was to write marketing material for our new headquarters.

Chapter 58

My writing had been praised in school and I had no difficulty creating the marketing material. But it *was* hard describing what we did since *The Company*, which is what its employees call it, performed both open and discreet activities.

The publicized ones dealt with security. We provided bodyguards and investigated employee backgrounds. Our clandestine work involved what governments wanted done with deniability. Like the permanent removal of threatening individuals or groups. The Company rendered Biblical justice at a time when few people read the Bible.

These activities weren't marketed. They were quietly requested from one of our Directors. The Company's feared Firestorm Unit consists of former Special Forces soldiers from the United States, Great Britain, and Russia. Their armament include Heckler & Koch G36 5.56x45mm assault rifles with 100-round-drum magazines, Spike-MR (medium range) and LR (long range) portable "fire-and-forget" missiles, and Scalable Offensive Hand Grenades which can be "stacked" to boost blast power.

Their transportation is provided by Boeing AH-64E attack helicopters fitted with fire control radar, 30-mm cannon, and anti-tank guided missiles.

The Company had protected Erika's billionaire family for a decade. Through Vladimir I had become steeped in its lore and engaged in behavior which many would deem criminal though others would term saintly.

"There is the justice of lawyers and the courtroom, and the justice of The Prophets and of God," is The Company creed.

Margaret: Mother of Twins

Company activities had endangered me in Tokyo and London and New York. What came next? I wondered, even as my children dozed in my arms.

Chapter 59

"We were almost *arrested*," my oldest sister, Melody, said.

Her smile seemed inappropriate but I was used to her ways. She would soon begin law school but, being a long-term movie buff, her heart lay in Hollywood.

"What happened?" I asked.

"Jessica's bachelorette party."

"Yes?"

I waited patiently. Melody told stories by her own clock. It did no good to try to speed her along.

"We wanted to make her sendoff special, something she'd never forget."

"And you did."

"You might say that."

I felt the frequent sensations of mothers: tired, tried, and losing patience

"Please," I pleaded.

"OK. We held her bridezilla party at the Hilton, wearing matching Bride Squad shirts, tiaras, and sashes."

"That doesn't sound bad. Why were you almost arrested?" I asked.

"We rented a tractor to pull a flatbed trailer. It carried us dancing and chanting 'I was never a virgin' while holding beers over our heads. One of us had an inflatable hat with a foot long penis. Traffic backed up."

"I see," I said, coolly.

Mothers, even young ones, look down on such foolishness. While beer isn't a permitted beverage for our Mormon family, this was her personal choice. But Melody's arrest would be a family issue. It would impact her future and that of our father who was a Connecticut Supreme Court judge.

"You *almost* got arrested," I said, becoming instantly alert and wanting to know more.

"Stop worrying! It didn't happen since the police knew our families. We were warned and sent down a side road to stop holding up traffic. They were nice enough to escort us back to the hotel."

I exhaled and said nothing. Just like kids, adults sometimes act dopy.

"Our next bridezilla will be in Vegas where anything goes," she said.

"That's a good idea," I agreed.

My phone rang and I reached for it. I had been expecting Vladimir's call with more instructions but it wasn't him. The screaming voice was female.

Chapter 60

"Murdered!" cried Enid.

I had last heard that word when Venla, Erika's Finnish stepsister, was distraught over the killing of wolves in Finland. It took me a moment to catch my bearings.

"Tell me what happened," I said calmly.

Being cool during an emergency came naturally after the risky experiences that I had survived.

"Francis was shot yesterday evening. I just saw it on the news," Enid said.

Though considering the death of her Mafia lover to be good news, I didn't say this. My thoughtlessness has its limit and I exuded sympathy.

"You must be really down," I said, softly.

"My life is over. I don't know what to do. I have no one," Enid said.

While the death of a loved one is hardest on the survivor, it need not crush their life. People are tough but saying this wouldn't help.

"You had good years together and have memories," I steeled myself to say. "And you do have us. Joanne and Vera are both widows. You have your therapist too,"

"I stopped seeing him," Enid said.

"Oh?"

"Last week. He pressed me to stop seeing Francis."

"You do have us," I repeated.

"Can I see you now? There are regular trains and I'll come to Greenwich," Enid asked.

I had wanted to be alone with my babies but didn't feel able to refuse. No more than a Girl Scout leader could reject a Brownie's tearful plea And I knew that sometimes, when words fail, just being there is enough.

"OK, come this afternoon. Call and let me know when you're arriving. I'll ask Erika to pick you up at the station. If she can't make it, you can come by taxi," I said, and gave her my address.

I then left a message on Maria's phone stating that I needed her to babysit after school. She could use the money and I wanted more than Mila present when Enid came. What do you really know about her? I asked myself. Only what she told us, came the uneasy reply.

Chapter 61

Maria looked happier than when we last met. Maybe she has a new boyfriend, I thought, but didn't ask. She was my employee and not my child, I reminded myself.

Erika delivered Enid and Mila brought them to the children's playroom where I had been writing. I looked up, feeling drunk with my word creation. Their clothes caught my attention and Maria openly stared. Perhaps it was my misperception but I thought that my babies did too.

Erika's old-time style had been brought up-to-date. With its high-neck and ruffles, think nineteen-hundred Kansas meets Nordstrom. Though more chic than country sweet, it aroused memories of a rustic past when wives churned butter and baked bread. I didn't ask the cost of her outfit. A thousand dollars was my estimate.

Enid's stunning red/blue/orange clothing seemed too colorful for grieving but this bitchy thought might have derived from jealousy. Bottega Veneta sweater, Gucci dress, Hermes strap and shawl, Missoni striped scarf, and MSGM sneakers don't come from Walmart.

After moments of mutual admiration, Enid and Erika sat beside me. With one on each side, I felt like a mother who must divide her attention between siblings. Being unsure what to say, I waited. Enid looked too cheerful for the widow-supportive comments that had populated my mind before her arrival.

I had already learned from Vera and Joanne that the usual widow feels frozen: too fragile to face reality and make changes while absorbing their trauma. But Enid looked serene. Apart from being twenty-five and her Mafia lover having just been murdered, I knew nothing about her. Not the work she did or where she came from. It was time to find out.

Chapter 62

"Your outfit is *very* attractive," I said.

I really wanted was to ask how she could afford it but didn't. People tell the truth when they're ready, my lawyer-father often said. Enid seemed to expect my question.

"My work pays well," she said, demurely.

"What do you do?" I asked.

"I help people."

"*You help people,*" I repeated, slowly.

"Yes, I'm an accountant and help people with their finances."

"Huh." I said.

People like to boast and information is often gained by acting stupid. This is more of my dad's advice.

"Francis trained me. That's also why I'm grateful to him," Enid said.

Erika took up the charge, sensing the information that I wanted.

"He must have been quite a guy," she said.

Enid leaned back and smiled.

"Could I have coffee. Black with sugar?" she asked.

"Sure."

"The same with cream," requested Erika.

While Mormons consider coffee unhealthy and don't indulge, they don't impose their beliefs onto others. A business manager must socialize and many people want coffee. My kitchen holds the coffee-maker that one finds in the better auto dealerships.

I was back in a few minutes. The elegant Madame Recoit pattern tray held coffee in two cups of the same design, a glass of milk for me, and Pepperidge Farm Farmhouse Dark Chocolate Chip Cookies. The gourmet Smiley Face and Heart cookies, from Greenwich's celebrated St. Moritz Bakery, I save for children. With munchies beckoning, we settled down for what I hoped would be the truth and wasn't disappointed.

"Francis and I came from different worlds. My family's money is from banking and his was from... I never told you his last name," Enid said.

Her voice cracked as fear creased her youthful face. She spoke the name softly, almost in a whisper. I immediately understood and so the others.

Chapter 63

Francis' last name hadn't been O'Donnell or Dietrich or Cohen. This I knew since Mafia members rarely had non-Italian members though some long past notables were Jewish and Irish. It was an Italian surname which is known to all Americans.

Francis' father had been murdered in a well-publicized gangland hit. There was speculation why but no really knew. With his death, the gang's management passed to an uncle, Francis not being considered vicious enough to control it, according to Enid.

"He was a sweetie," she said.

Neither Erika nor I smiled, as befit our good self-control.

"So what kind of work do you do?" Erika asked.

Erika's father owns hedge funds and had tutored her since childhood. Her business knowledge far surpassed mine.

Enid sipped coffee, replaced the cup on the tray, and leaned back. She's about to tell us the whole story, I sensed, though increasingly feeling that I didn't want to hear it. Being supportive of grieving widows and a worried tenant is one thing. Learning crime secrets can lead to trouble.

"I'd experimented with pot but generally been prudish in high school. Thinking that the kids who did heroin were crazy, even when their faces looked ecstatic with the rush. I both scorned and envied them. I'd been miserable at a party and wanted to be happy again. Temptation overcame fear.

"No one forced me and friends told me not to. But I felt that if I didn't try smack, I would be more lost than I already was. I planned to use it just once, to jump the chasm and test myself."

Chapter 64

Enid continued her story, now with tear-filled eyes.

"My boyfriend insisted that he didn't want me to do it but smiled as he fixed the injection. I could hardly believe that in a moment I'd have taken heroin but it seemed what I wanted. When he released my arm after the sting of the needle, I licked away the blood and he gave me a congratulatory kiss. I felt sleepy and proud.

"If I'd stopped then, things would have been OK but I felt that I had to do it again before I could say I'd really done heroin. I didn't get the chemical rush which users speak of. It's like with pot where you must do it a few times before feeling the effects. An internal barrier must be crossed before the chemical awakens the nerves.

"The next week I felt a happy thrill and dreaminess and warmth. Now, I think this might not have been from the drug but from feeling gutsy at using it.

"At first, things were fine. I grinned with pleasure, asking myself why I hesitated. Two weeks later I found that I couldn't stop using. All our group's thoughts revolved about Harry, the dealer, and when he'd arrive with his packets of pleasure. While waiting for him, our silly conversation took more and more effort.

"We giggled at how our eyes looked and gloried in our secret, soon-to-come calm and feeling that we were the most beautiful people in the world.

"We split the drug's cost between us. Money wasn't a problem until my rich parents grilled me about the red points on my skin and studied my eyes."

Chapter 65

"Heroin calmed me and smoothed my faults. With it, I was the most beautiful girl in the world. Sex was ecstatic and my boyfriend and I made love for hours.

"At first my parents were in denial but when my grades dropped, they cut my weekly allowance from a hundred to twenty dollars. My mother screamed, 'Do you even know what you're doing?'

"I didn't and was too strung out to care. My other friends deserted me when they learned. At school during a TV program about the heroin trade, I blurted, 'It's a good experience. I've done it.' I got a strange look and left, deciding that I needed new friends.

"A week later, I was sitting outdoors at a coffee shop reading an accounting text. Vito sat himself at a neighboring table. He smiled, looked at the book, and said that he worked in finance too. He looked like money so I smiled back and let him pick me up.

"He must have sensed I used drugs and was hungry for it. Like a mechanic can simply hear an engine and know something is wrong. Vito lived in a condo near Battery Park and we drove there in his Porsche. He had smack and I stayed."

My mothering instinct overcame me.

"Didn't your parents worry?" I asked.

"They were beyond that. I called and said I would be staying with a girl-friend a few weeks. I have three sisters and am easily overlooked."

Enid sipped more coffee and became silent. The only sound in the room came from my infants. They were far too young to understand Enid's story but I noted Maria listening closely.

"What happened then?" Erika asked.

"I became Vito's whore, a girlfriend to be shared with his friends and customers," Enid said, remorsefully but with a fake smile.

Chapter 66

"Why did you stay with Vito?" Erika asked calmly.

"Have either of you done smack?" she asked, rhetorically.

We shook our heads simultaneously.

"You find yourself doing what you couldn't imagine. I craved heroin and Vito had it," Enid said.

"What happened?" I asked.

"He beat me when I wanted out. That was on the day he introduced me to Francis at a party."

Enid sipped more coffee before continuing.

"Vito joked, 'she's also an accountant.' Francis quizzed me when we were alone, asking about my family and how I wound up with Vito. I sensed he really wanted to know me and not just fuck. So I told him everything, including that my drug use now included cocaine.

"He said that his business needed a smart, well-bred accountant and if I worked for him, he would help me get off drugs and I would make more money than I could imagine. I thought what he said might have been bullshit but he was persuasive and I bought it.

"Vito didn't want to lose me but he had no choice. Francis might not have been considered tough enough to run the gang but he was plenty tough. He paid for my rehab and I got clean."

"Did you stay clean?" I asked, knowing how difficult this is.

"Yes. Francis gave me the best motive. He said that he'd kill me if I used drugs again and I believed him," Enid replied.

"And you never did," I said, softly.

"I've been dumb but never suicidal," Enid said.

"You were never dumb," Erika said, supportively.

"I was about using drugs and letting Vito pick me up. Joining with Francis wasn't dumb," Enid said, assuredly.

Mila had been sitting apart from us, listening from her comfortable wing chair. Before becoming a bodyguard, she had been a Russian Special Forces doctor and, earlier, a police officer. Now she spoke for the first time.

"Tell us what you did for Francis," she said, in a commanding tone.

Chapter 67

"The work I did with Francis? Why do you want to know?" Enid asked.

Her tone registered suspicion and I wondered too. Mila's voice had indicated more than curiosity.

Mila leaned forward. Her look was one of a mother needing to explain a threat to a clueless child but she kept her cool.

"Enid, you don't know me but I am responsible for the safety of Margaret and her children. For this reason, I must insist that you never come here again and have no further contact with the women's group. These demands aren't negotiable but I do have a suggestion that may save your life."

I broke the silence that followed. Mila and I have different personalities. My protective shell consists of humor and sarcasm. Her's is of withdrawal and contained fury. Only then did I recognize the danger that my action had caused my family.

"I've been dumb, haven't I?" I asked, rhetorically.

Mila nodded agreement while waiting for Enid's response. To her credit she instantly understood.

"You're saying that those who killed Francis know I worked with him. That I'm next in their sights together with whoever I may have shared our work with," Enid said.

In reply, Mila spoke a proverb, first in Russian and then its English translation.

"This is written with pitchfork on flowing water. An American would say, nobody knows whether it will happen or not."

To which I added my word of advice, "Safety first!"

"Amen," said Erika.

The children's noise reminded me of Maria's presence. She has already heard too much, I thought. I made a mental note to speak with her before she left and turned toward her.

"Maria, it's nearly their naptime. Please put them to bed," I ordered.

She smiled and silently obeyed, likely having grasped my motive: that she shouldn't hear what Enid would reveal. I wouldn't have hired Maria if she were stupid.

Chapter 68

Enid pointed her empty coffee cup toward me. I regarded this as rude but, without a word, took it to refill and returned a few minute later. Silent communication had become a staple of this conversation.

After taking several sips, Enid told what Mila asked. Though probably not everything, it was enough to arouse alarm.

"Francis was more clever than smart. He could choose a profitable fraud but not know how to do it. He needed someone with knowledge to front for him, an ally who looked like they came from money and not the streets. He looked like a thug.

"We had several businesses. One involved offshore finance and another was stealing bitcoins. I ran the first business but was only indirectly involved with the second. I'm good at math and computers but that one was way outside my league.

"A financial offshore specialist manages shell companies, shuffling money around the world to avoid taxes or launder criminal earnings. For doing this we were paid two-percent of the assets we moved. It was very profitable."

Enid paused to sip her coffee.

"How much money were you handling?" Mila asked.

"That depended. Three-hundred-forty-million dollars during our first year. Last year it was a little over eleven-billion-dollars."

"That isn't chicken-feed," said Erika.

Margaret: Mother of Twins

"Nor is it a recipe for long life," said Mila, coldly. Her look toward Enid wasn't friendly.

Chapter 69

I became increasingly nervous. The crimes which Enid described weren't small-potatoes. She and Francis had been involved with powerful people as his murder proved. To help Enid avoid the same fate, a situation which she didn't yet fully seem to grasp, more information was needed.

"Please describe the bitcoin theft and where you laundered the stolen funds," Mila said, in a soft yet demanding tone.

Enid understood that Mila's courteous words shouldn't be ignored. She replaced her coffee cup on the table and nestled in the thickly cushioned sofa. Her move was like my father's before telling a good story and Enid's tale didn't disappoint.

"The value of a bitcoin quickly exploded from a hundred-dollars to fourteen-thousand-dollars when we started. It presented an unpoliced digital forest ripe for the taking. Francis saw this opportunity before anyone but couldn't do it alone.

"I knew only enough technology to understand cryptocurrency. To succeed, we needed an accomplice and Francis ordered me to find them. I was the honey-trap pushed amongst the queen bees. The biology is wrong but you get my point," Enid said.

We did.

"I began my search in Cyprus. Its banks are wide-open with few questions being asked. We had used them to funnel stolen money into European Union countries. I hung around computer cafes, wearing skirts which inched shorter by the day."

Enid smiled, as if she were reliving that excitement.

"Ross was brilliant and desperate. His fingers skimmed over the computer keyboard like a virtuoso pianist making beautiful music. I leaned close, he turned and his head brushed against my hip. I begged his help to send E-mail. It was the beginning of a beautiful relationship like they say in the movies."

Chapter 70

"I flirted and invited Ross to my room where I learned his story. He had once been clean but never kosher, as they say. He'd been expelled from MIT after selling cocaine in a dorm. His father was an big donor so the school kept it quiet.

"After returning home in disgrace, his family tried tough love by throwing him out with a five-thousand-dollar check. They said he could only return when he was 'clean and working.'

"Ross' only marketable skill was hacking so he did that, getting jobs on the internet's Dark Web. He also did legitimate stuff including contract work for the FBI if you can believe it.

"After tiring of living in a furnished room and using coffee shop Wi-Fi, he left the country to seek his fortune but mostly more. Despite being good-looking, he never had a relationship lasting longer than a month. He's what you might call, *socially challenged.*

"Ross flew to Stockholm, having heard that their women are the loosest. He stayed there a few months, supporting himself by handling the computers of a local drug gang. 'I don't discriminate. I'll work for whoever pays me whether it's the FBI or who they chase,' he joked. After hearing this, I knew that he'd be perfect for us.

"When the gang that Ross was working for got busted, he fled to Cyprus which is a money-laundering hub. Fearing that he had only days before being arrested and extradited to Sweden, returning to America with me seemed an ideal solution.

"Taking Ross onboard would be Francis' decision so I phoned him. He agreed that Ross sounded good: we had both been druggies, he was desperate, a crook at heart, and he loved me."

"Weren't you afraid that Francis would be jealous?" Erika asked.

"Why? I never said a word about his wife or objected to the other women he fucked," Enid replied, with surprise.

Despite being flaky, Enid has a strong logical streak, I thought.

Chapter 71

"What *exactly* did Ross do?" Mila asked.

"Besides fucking me?" Enid responded, with a mischievous smile.

Mila waved her hand disapprovingly and Enid nodded acceptance of the scolding.

"In order to understand you'll have to know some things. Unlike paper money, a bitcoin only exists online as a string of code in a digital ledger called a blockchain. Being apart from the normal financial system, it's ideal for crimes: selling stolen credit cards and weapons or getting a ransom payment after hacking the computer system of a hospital," Enid began.

"The bitcoin's digital ledger is kept by masses of computers around the world. They assure that a person can't use the same bitcoin to pay for something more than once. Bitcoin *addresses* are identified by strings of letters and numbers with the names of the owners being hidden.

"In theory, a bank or credit-card company isn't needed to ensure the validity of interactions since the blockchain does that. But in practice, bitcoins move through *exchanges* with Tokyo's Mt. Cox being one of the first and largest.

"Mt. Cox served as a platform to buy and sell bitcoins, maintaining the users' password-protected digital wallets where the bitcoins are stored. Ross consumed dozens of Cokes and bags of Fritos while working day and night. I helped by massaging his shoulders. He was too obsessed with work to think about sex.

"He sat facing four monitors: one with lines of code, another to record vital information, a third to write notes, and a fourth for video gaming to relax. He succeeded in writing a program to access the private keys and steal bitcoins from the digital wallets. The proceeds from these sales were sent to banks in Cyprus and Latvia that he had worked with before.

"Everything went well until it suddenly didn't. Bitcoins have no practical use in commerce so their value is driven by momentum trading and not fundamentals. Their value crashed, online thieves were being arrested, and we ended this scheme to begin a new fraud."

Chapter 72

"Our last fraud involved swapping SIMs, the Subscriber Identification Module. SIM cards verify subscribers on mobile phones. Our fraud consisted of tricking a phone company into transferring a subscriber's phone number to a SIM card controlled by us. We then reset the subscriber's passwords and stole from their online bank accounts," Enid said.

"How many did you access?" Erika asked.

"Twenty-nine, mostly of corrupt Balkan officials. It worked well until security companies issued a warning," Enid replied.

"You were a busy threesome," I murmured.

"Just doing business," Enid said, with a small smile.

Her comment floored me but I kept my mouth shut.

"What do you plan to do now?" I asked.

"Enjoy life. I'm financially independent and Greenwich is attractive. Maybe I'll buy a house here, one with a swimming pool and tennis court, of course," Enid said, again with a smile.

"Where did Ross go?" Mila asked.

"I don't know. I haven't been able to contact him. He's not answering his phone."

He might have been killed when they killed Francis, I thought, but then wasn't the moment to say. Enid was too hopped up with her sudden wealth and independence and wouldn't listen. I changed the subject.

"What did Francis look like?" I asked, wondering what had attracted Enid to him besides his money.

Without a word, she took a photo from her wallet. Francis was in his late-thirties. His face had high prominent cheekbones and was both handsome and ugly. The deep ridges of his forehead and heavy grooves in his cheeks revealed hard living. Lines ran from the nose to the chin, enclosing full sensual lips. The receding wavy brown hair lent a devilish touch. From beneath dark brows, clear blue eyes looked forth with the wariness of a jungle animal. The man radiated self-assurance.

"He was a handsome man," I said.

"I loved him. He loved me and trusted me and now he's gone," Enid said.

With that statement, she seemed to crumple.

Chapter 73

Enid turned away to conceal her anguish.

"All that caffeine. Where's the bathroom," she asked, getting up.

"I'll show you," I said.

We need to speak alone and this will be a good time, I thought.

Doing her thing took a long time and I feared that she might have taken a drug. As it turned out, she simply needed time to pull herself together. Cosmetics help and she looked better as she approached me.

"We have to talk. Let's go to my room," I said.

Though she was older, I took charge and she followed.

When we were comfortably seated, I told her the facts.

"You're in danger and need protection. Francis is dead and probably Ross too. Another murder won't matter to the killers," I said.

Despite my words and severe tone, I hadn't gotten through to her. She merely smiled, as one would to calm a crazy relative. Then I remembered what my lawyer-father once told me: that to convince a person with an opposing point of view, you must make the situation personal by telling them a story. I did, and it may have worked because my story was so terrible.

"I've been in your situation," I began.

This statement captured Enid's attention and I continued.

"Several years ago, in Tokyo, I was helping to rescue a kidnapped child from a monster. Things didn't work out as planned and I was taken prisoner. I lay naked, tied to a table as he approached with a soldering iron. Facing me was a video monitor showing him torturing another girl."

I paused to let my words sink in. Enid's smile was gone.

"If he was prepared to work me over with a soldering iron just because he felt betrayed, imagine what would be done to you if information were sought," I said.

Her next statement revealed that I *had* reached her.

"I *am* afraid. Ross is probably dead and I'm next," Enid admitted.

"Why," I asked.

"He knew only the technical stuff. I handled the money and Francis provided the muscle when needed. People feared him, not us," Enid said.

"He's dead," I said.

"Yes, but I have our money and records," Enid said.

"Records?" I asked.

"Of bribed government officials and tax frauds. It's deadly stuff," Enid replied.

The word "deadly" hung in the air. That was the moment when I *really* took charge and became a boss.

"As I see it, you have two huge problems: saving your life and staying out of prison. Do you want my help?" I asked, with an assurance that astonished me.

"Yes."

"Private protection is expensive," I warned.

"Cost isn't an issue. Francis trusted me with everything and I would never have betrayed him," Enid said.

"OK. I have to make a call. Don't leave this room," I ordered.

Then I went to my home-office, to try to keep my promises.

Chapter 74

Vladimir picked up on the second ring and I quickly explained the situation. He promised to reassign two bodyguards to my house from Erika's for temporary service. Their replacements would fly from Berlin the next day.

"How do you plan to handle her legal issues?" he asked.

"She holds valuable files: evidence of political bribes, tax evasion, and money-laundering throughout Europe and Africa. Many governments would overlook much for just a peek," I replied.

"You used good judgment. She should leave the country quickly. I could arrange for her new British or German or Russian passport and passage. Tell me which country she would prefer and send me her photo," Vladimir ordered.

"I felt sure you would help," I said.

We understood each other perfectly. Vladimir had high-level contacts in Moscow and among our company directors were retired CIA and MI6 officials. The value of Enid's files lay in their power to blackmail.

Enid was sprawled on the chaise lounge in my bedroom when I returned. She looked thoughtful.

"They had no chance," she said.

"Who?"

"Francis and Ross. Francis grew up in a Mafia family and Ross was jailed for being too honest as a teenager. That and drugs sent him down the wrong path," Enid said.

"Ross' story sounds interesting," I said.

"It is. As a kid he liked to play with electronic stuff. His mother hated it."

"That happens," I said, hesitantly.

"After she smashed his Nintendo, Ross tried to fix it. He learned how it worked and went on to computers. When his family was vastly overcharged on their phone bill and his mother's complaint got nowhere, he hacked into the phone company's network, accidentally crashing its East Coast operations. Then he made the mistake of being honest."

"What was that?"

"He called the phone company and said that if they corrected his mother's bill, he would tell how he hacked them. They called the police and the usual happened. Being a nerdy guy, he was terrified of jail but the prisoners protected him. They wanted to be his friend since a brilliant hacker would be a great crime asset after they were released.

"The irony is that the phone company lost a class-action lawsuit because of its billing errors. Ross' mother got a refund but he had a felony conviction."

"If you're convicted of a crime you didn't commit, you may as well commit it," I said.

"Now you're whistling Dixie," Enid said, having recovered her cool.

Then I told her how my company intended to keep her safe and out of prison.

Chapter 75

"The stolen files can save you. Are they secure?" I asked.

"Ross used the same security standard that the government uses to protect its secrets. AES-256 encrypted copies are on three USB drives. You need a password to read them," Enid said.

"Is the password secure?"

"It's not written anywhere. I memorized it."

"Did Francis or Ross know it?" I pressed.

"No. Francis never dealt with the technical stuff and Ross said it would be best if only I knew it. Unfortunately, he was right," Enid said.

Her eyes filled with tears and I waited before continuing.

"Where are the drives?" I asked.

"I've always carried them, in case I'd have to run someday," Enid said.

"The money is secure too?" I asked.

"In foreign numbered accounts that I can access by computer. Money isn't an issue," Enid said.

I nodded approval. Despite her Valley Girl style, I had been right to believe that she thought logically.

"You must become anonymous and leave the country quickly. We can supply you with a British, German, or Russian passport. Your protection could be guaranteed by those nations. Which would you prefer?" I asked.

"Not America?" Enid asked.

"Arranging that would take too long. It would require agreement between the FBI and the Justice Department with nothing being certain. An officious government lawyer might feel that, regardless of the value of your files, you should serve jail time. The other countries' services are more flexible," I said.

"Germany, then. I studied there for a term and am fairly fluent though no one would believe me a native. You could name me Brunilda but I would prefer something nicer. Eva?" Enid asked, with a smile.

That she possessed so many qualities surprised me.

"You're quite a woman," I said.

"That's what Francis often said."

This time she didn't hold back the tears.

Chapter 76

"You'll stay here until your passport and travel arrangements arrive," I said.

Enid nodded agreement so I went on.

"Two bodyguards have been reassigned here from Erika's home. One will stay by your side and the other will be nearby. I have an extra bedroom you can use. We're about the same size and you can take some of my clothes. Your's are too noticeable," I added.

Enid nodded compliance. She'll be a perfect client, I hoped.

Looking down over her dress she said, in a sad tone, "I'll have to become a new person, never to wear such clothes again. I'll feel lost."

"Your life has changed. Vladimir will take charge when you arrive in Berlin. You'll like him. He helps people change their lives and be safe. Cheer up! Where no one knows you, everything awaits you," I said.

"I'll remember that. I have a lot to learn," she said.

"Now I'll teach you something else," I said.

My babies were awake and hungry when I entered their room. Maria was doing her homework close by. Both would get a learning experience which I felt proud to be able to give. Every mother was once a novice and I had been taught to breastfeed by an experienced nurse. My lesson would be a life-affirming experience for Enid, soon to be secreted as Eva.

"Gather round. You're about to get some hard-learned instruction," I said, playfully.

"The first thing to know about breast-feeding is that an infant is an efficient suction machine. But to turn your breasts into drinking fountains requires that you get it right. The first time you'll have no idea what to do. It'll be like when your mom handed you a tampon at your first period."

I picked up James and continued.

"You hold the child low and behind their ears. Then, using your entire hand, you guide his head onto your breast. Your baby can't yet control his head and won't be able to without your help. By brushing your nipple against his mouth, instinct will cause him to *root*. A newborn opens their mouth if any part of their face is touched," I explained.

Enid looked entranced and Maria looked surprised. Her part-time job had turned out to be far different than she expected.

"What if you have flat nipples?" Enid asked.

I felt pleased that her mind was now off her danger.

"That won't be a problem. A baby doesn't get milk by sucking on the nipple but by sucking on the areola tissue, the darkened area behind the nipple. If breastfeeding is painful, it's because the mother hasn't gotten their baby's mouth far enough onto her breast."

With that, I ended my lesson and concentrated on satisfying my babies.

Chapter 77

Enid and Maria had watched me closely, soaking up critical knowledge for their future days as a mother. When finished, I left Maria to do her homework and showed Enid to the bedroom she would occupy until leaving. I pointed out the toiletries, repeated that she should freely partake of my clothes, and took her digital photo for her new passport. After E-mailing the photo to Vladimir there was nothing to do but wait.

Before returning downstairs, I popped into the children's room to speak with Maria. My serious look made her nervous.

"Did I do something wrong?" she asked, with a worried expression.

"No, you're a wonderful babysitter. It's something else. The security business that I manage requires confidentiality. Who we work with and what you learn while working here must remain here. It must not be shared with your mother or friends or anyone else. Can you follow this?" I asked.

"I can keep my mouth shut," Maria said.

"Including about who visits?"

"You had visitors?"

"*Very good*," I said slowly. Then, "How is your mother's search for work going?"

"It's gone nowhere. She hasn't found house-cleaning customers to replace those who've moved. She can't seem to operate in the new economy where employers hire online and not by word-of-mouth recommendation," Maria said.

"I can use a reliable housekeeper particularly since I'll have overnight guests. They'll be mostly Utah relatives but also an occasional business customer needing a private place. My home-office and the office downtown also need cleaning. Would your mother consider working full-time for me? She'd be well-paid and get corporate benefits including health insurance for your family. But she'll have to pass a background check," I said.

"That wouldn't be a problem. She would love a steady job. Bless you," Enid said, with teary eyes.

"Good. Have her call me," I said.

Erika was putting on her jacket when I arrived downstairs.

"I've got to go. Clarence wants me with him at his doctor's appointment," Erika said.

Her boyfriend's diabetes required regular medical checkup.

"I'm sorry to have taken so long. It took time to get things worked out," I said.

"When in a hurry, you should work slowly and methodically," Erika said.

I stood shocked, once again being floored by her astuteness. But all I said was what Francis had told Enid: "You're quite a woman."

Chapter 78

It took three days for Enid's passport to arrive and her travel arrangements to be made. She was thoughtful during our last hours together.

"Can I ask two favors?" she asked, hesitantly.

"Absolutely."

She handed me a slip of paper.

"I haven't seen my family for years and may never be able to see them again. Will you call and say that I love them and am OK. That I'm doing secret work for the government and can't contact them directly.

"And if the worst happens, tell them that I died honorably serving our country. It's what parents want to hear about their soldier-kids when they die," Enid said.

"Absolutely!" I repeated, with watering eyes.

"Also, could I say 'goodbye' to James and Donna and be their far off aunt who sends occasional presents?" Enid pleaded.

"A child can never have too much love," I said, softly.

The children were not yet asleep when we entered their room. I brightened the night light as Enid went close to croon a two-hundred-year-old lullaby.

> Twinkle, twinkle, little star,
>
> How I wonder what you are!
>
> Up above the world so high,
>
> Like a diamond in the sky.

Margaret: Mother of Twins

When this blazing sun is gone,

When he nothing shines upon.

Then you show your little light,

Twinkle, twinkle, through the night.

Then the traveler in the dark,

Thanks you for your tiny spark.

He could not see where to go,

If you did not twinkle so.

In the dark blue sky you keep,

And often through my curtains peep,

For you never shut your eye

Till the sun is in the sky.

As your bright and tiny spark,

Lights the traveler in the dark,

Though I know not what you are,

Twinkle, twinkle, little star.

The bodyguards, who had brought her new German passport, watched as she sang. When finished, she silently accompanied them to the waiting car for the short ride to

Westchester Airport. Their private flight would reach Berlin at dawn.

Chapter 79

The household grew. Maria's mother, Annette, was hired, and with her came Maria's young brother as an occasional visitor.

Annette was a conscientious worker. Even I, who had become obsessively tidy, quickly noticed the difference. My home became the pleasure that it was when I first moved in. Her presence also freed my time to become a passable cook. "Every mother is *that*," my youngest sister insisted, and I took her claim to heart.

Though having long believed that cooking well required a gene which I lacked, I discovered this isn't true. Achieving good results only required following recipes and patience. But I often lacked the latter.

I had imagined a corporate manager's life to be different. Having been lulled by viewing relaxed bosses in movies, I believed that would be my experience too but it wasn't. *They* didn't have two infants and work from home. *They* didn't have a household to oversee. *They* didn't have a teenage babysitter with regularly changing romances.

You can do it, I told myself, and I did.

Things became easier when Jordan returned from Berlin, newly hired and hungry to work. Despite my initial concern at being younger and a woman, these didn't bother him. He related to me as he had to his superiors in the Army though I insisted that he address me as "Margaret." Ours is an informal company and only Vladimir isn't spoken of by their first name or nickname. All address him by his former military rank of "General."

"That always happens when high-ranking officers retire to jobs," Jordan said.

He spent most of his time in our new office. We met there every Friday to discuss concerns and new business opportunities. Our meetings were relaxed and began with family chitchat. One day it didn't and he seemed nervous. His question startled me and my response was slow in coming.

"Are we killers?" he asked.

Chapter 80

"Are we killers? That's an odd question. I like things to be out in the open. What's on your mind?" I asked.

My reasonable tone calmed him and Jordan sipped his coffee before speaking. It was Jamaica Blue Mountain Reserve, an expensive brand that gourmets loved. I didn't drink it but a boss must please others to stay in business.

"That came out wrong. Elizabeth had a difficult night," he said, apologetically.

Eliozabeth was his pregnant wife.

"No offense taken but what's your concern?" I asked, leaning forward.

"I like your father," Jordan said.

"Vladimir can be a charmer."

"Yes. He took me to a party where I met people from MAD (*Militärischer Abschirimdienst*, German's military counterintelligence service). They told me stories about you and your Russian uncle, Borya, an intelligence official nicknamed Lucifer (The Devil)."

"You shouldn't believe everything that you hear. Most gossip isn't true," I said.

"What *is* the truth?" Jordan asked.

I sipped milk before answering. The entire truth wasn't something that I wanted to reveal nor need he learn. But my answer had to satisfy him lest he quit. And an angry ex-employee can damage a company, even one who signed a non-disclosure agreement upon hiring.

"The company is owned by three people: my father, Vladimir, who is a former Russian general; a retired senior official of the CIA; and a retired, highly honored member of the British Secret Service. It has two divisions. One provides conventional security services for wealthy people and government officials. The other offers paramilitary services for Western governments and only them. These are mostly the United States, Great Britain, and Germany. They can conduct these operations on their own but hire us when seeking deniability.

"Nothing, and I repeat, nothing, that the company engages in would impinge your honor as a West Point graduate. Unless you object to such things as rescuing those who've been kidnapped. Our action people are former Special Forces soldiers from Russia, Great Britain, or the United States. A retired official of the Texas Rangers is another employee.

"You will never be asked to do anything criminal. If a person requests this, as to murder a troublesome spouse, we would report them to the appropriate authorities. Does this answer your question?" I asked.

Jordan smiled for the first time that morning.

"Completely. But tell me, did you really stop a bioterror attack on West Point by yourself?"

"Who told you that?"

"Borya."

"He loves me and exaggerates. Like I said, you shouldn't believe everything you hear," I said, with a smile.

Chapter 81

Jordan settled into our East Coast business which, largely, didn't yet exist. Security services aren't marketed like cars but sought through word-of-mouth recommendation. Using a promotion slogan as, *When in danger, we protect better*, wouldn't work.

Favorable notice is gained subtly by giving talks and attending conferences. Jordan's military background and West Point contacts helped. I encouraged him to widen his network even as his wife advised how to dress. She recognized that military life, in which your body belongs to the service, is poor preparation for the civilian workplace.

I supported her effort by instituting a new perk for company officers: a clothing allowance of five-thousand-dollars a year. The company's eagle-eyed accountant in Berlin questioned this but Vladimir backed me. He understood the military.

Thereafter, I gave no further instructions to Jordan. None were needed for we both knew that without new customers, we would be out of a job.

Jordan had much to learn about salesmanship. Erika's father, Hamilton ("call me Harry"), put him in touch with a top salesman of one of his companies. "Sales techniques are similar no matter what product is sold," Harry said.

Meanwhile, my learning continued. I became better at expressing breast milk after speaking with a nurse in my obstetrician's office.

"Don't use a bulb, the type that suctions milk from breasts with each squeeze. They're difficult to clean and cause sore nipples. I recommend an electric pump, despite its cost ranging from the hundreds to a thousand dollars. It's fast, easy to use, and leaves a mother's hands free for nursing on the other breast or another activity while pumping. It's not movable but you can get a portable pump for the road."

So that's what I did and my babies flourished.

Chapter 82

My women's group provided me with relief from everyday tasks. I had expressed milk for my babies and, despite my ever-present worry, turned their care over to their grandmother and Maria for the day. Jordan tended to his pregnant wife on Saturdays or doing whatever. The weekends belonged to them. I wouldn't contact him then except for an emergency which, since we hadn't gotten new business, wasn't likely to happen.

Randy's studies continued well and, though still a year from graduation, he had already been courted by high-tech companies, the National Security Agency, the Defense Intelligence Agency, the CIA, and the FBI. Despite generous offers, he intended a relaxed academic career which was my hope too. I wanted six babies even if most people consider this abnormal.

Except for some religious groups, few couples today have more than two children. So why, at twenty years of age and unmarried, did I crave more? After discussion with my mother, I concluded that I wanted six children for the following reasons.

Because James and Donna had improved my life by bringing me a special joy and more children would do the same.

Because, though tired, I wasn't yet wiped-out and was healthy.

Because some women *should* have more children to replace the aging population and make up for those who don't.

Because six children wouldn't have been considered unusual a hundred years ago when this size family was common.

Finally, *because* no matter how my work life turned out, my children would always keep me busy and give me a feeling of purpose.

"Have you asked Randy if he wants six children?" my mother asked.

"He's too busy for that discussion now. I'll persuade him one by one," I said, assuredly.

We both smiled.

Chapter 83

I couldn't fail to explain Enid's absence from the group. Though just beginning, its members had already bonded. She had been one of us. Now she and the drama of her life were gone. What should I say? How much could I say? I asked myself. Not the truth, I decided, before confronting the issue head-on.

"Enid has left the group. Not because she didn't value it but because we helped her so well that her problem was solved. She's left her boyfriend, to live with her family who is now abroad," I said.

The group took my news calmly. One can't feel deeply for someone who they barely knew. When no reaction came, to get their minds firmly off Enid, I spoke of my family-related activities since the last meeting: becoming better at breast-feeding, and decision to have six children. The business aspects of my life were off-limits here.

Smiles and silence followed as I turned toward Sam. Her fear that her landlord was a terrorist seemed the most pressing problem.

"Have you discovered more about your landlord? So far all we know is that she's congenial but has a nasty streak, has forgettable looks, and likes socializing with students." I said.

"I've been studying her though not openly of course. She let slip that she speaks German, French, and Arabic. She seems honest and emotionally transparent. Like being quick to say that a person is behaving thoughtlessly," Sam said.

"Not exactly the marks of a terrorist. Except for her language fluency, what you said could describe many," Joanne pressed.

"Isn't there *something* weird about her?" Krystal asked.

We waited as Sam thought for several moments.

"Her interest in bomb-making?" Sam asked, hesitantly.

Chapter 84

All eyes turned toward Sam.

"*Bomb making*?" Joanne repeated.

Her words hung in the air as Sam nodded.

"What makes you think this?" I asked.

"She has a huge monitor on her desk. The super came about a water leak and since she owns the apartment, I pushed into her bedroom without knocking and naturally glanced at the screen. 'Improvised Explosive Devices' was above the diagrams. She quickly blanked the screen and I told her about the water leak," Sam said.

"She also has a gun," Sam added, a moment later.

The silence in the room was deafening. Feeling it my duty as group leader to say something but being unsure what, I said simply, "Huh!" Then, after gathering my wits, I asked, "How do you know?"

"It was beside the monitor, with a can of oil and cleaning stuff," Sam said.

"You're observant," Krystal said.

"They stood out. I probably missed other things," Sam said.

Once again, I felt it my role to interrupt the silence.

"Sam's worry stretches our abilities and like the posters say, 'See something, Say something.' She has a sweet deal on her apartment but probably some government agency should be told. Even if frequent travel, reading about bomb-making, and having a gun don't make one a terrorist. I've traveled and own a pistol. Studying something shouldn't cause a person to be suspected of it. Writers investigate and Sam's landlord could work for a think tank or be writing a novel about college age terrorists. We don't know.

"I manage the American office of an international security firm. Let me run this by an expert and see what they suggest," I said.

My idea was accepted with a sense of relief.

"OK. Now, is there *another* crisis to be solved today?"

Though smiling and speaking with a comical tone, I hoped no one did. My Emotional Support Group seemed turning into a Crime Circle.

All looked down, like one did in school when afraid to be called on. Then Krystal spoke.

"My husband is trying to kill me," she said, slowly.

Chapter 85

Lawyers know about murder and Krystal was a lawyer so we took what she said seriously: that her husband is trying to kill her.

While divorcing people should behave maturely, this rarely happens. Instead, they enter the Wild-West of Family Court where financial execution and losing parental rights is a real possibility.

Some go crazy with a murdered spouse being the least that happens. In worse cases, the kids are murdered too and you've read these stories. It didn't take our questions to get Krystal talking.

"We've been together since high school and he was my only love. After college, he went to medical school and I studied law. I graduated first and supported our family during his Family Medicine residency.

"We both changed over the years. School wore us down and things got worse after our daughter was born. She was up nights with colic and he left me to do the parenting.

"He adopted expensive tastes after graduation, maybe feeling that he deserved it after years of struggle. Buying hand-made suits, hundred-dollar neckties, and a Porsche convertible. Our house was expensive, we were drowning in school debt, and Family Medicine has the lowest income. The specialists get the big bucks."

Krystal sipped coffee while deciding what to share next. She hadn't lost our attention.

"I was too involved with lawyering and our daughter to think about financial matters. Women can be stupid and particularly about those they love. But it was the money that blinded me," Krystal said, in a sober tone.

Chapter 86

"After a while, I *did* think that our finances made no sense. I wasn't making it and I didn't see how he could. I mean, how much does insurance pay for treating a kid's earache. It's not like he owned a super-profitable imaging machine clinic or something like that. I got furious when he bought a Harley. We both knew what ER doctors call motorcycle riders," Krystal said.

"Organ donors," I said, and she nodded.

She bit into her corned beef sandwich before continuing.

"This is *really* good!" she exclaimed.

"I ordered it from a Jewish deli the doorman recommended. I'll use them again," Erika promised, and Krystal continued.

"When he ignored my concern and said that riding relaxed him, what I said pissed him off royally: that he should triple his life insurance and sign a Do Not Resuscitate notice for when he's on life-support. That wasn't our only argument.

"The nurse he hired was a too pretty beginner and I began wondering if they had a thing going. He was coming home later than usual but doctors have ready excuses: 'there was an emergency' or 'I needed to make a house call.' It's to his credit that he makes house calls so few doctors do nowadays. But is it *her* house that he's calling at? I asked myself."

Krystal munched her sandwich before speaking again.

"By that time it didn't matter much since there was little going on between us apart from talking about our daughter and household stuff. There was nothing in bed. I was often asleep when he came home and he started sleeping in the guest bedroom. He said he didn't want to wake me but we both knew this was a lie."

Chapter 87

"What made you suspect that he might be cheating?" Jenna asked.

I was glad to see her healthy curiosity. While infidelity isn't something to be wished on anyone, it was more normal than what she endured while being sex trafficked.

Krystal finished her sandwich and picked up another. Her appetite surprised me. I would have none were I speaking about Randy cheating. But Krystal and her husband are separated and she has probably run countless scenarios of their relationship in her mind, I thought.

"Little things that mean nothing until they suddenly do. Phone calls ending when I entered the room. Lipstick on his collar which could have come from a relative. Late working hours that might have been true. But I couldn't explain the panties in his jacket when I took it to the cleaners," Krystal answered.

"You haven't considered that they might have been his?" Jenna asked.

Her mock-serious tone aroused the laugh that we needed.

"Maybe I should have," Krystal said, with a smile.

Being the group leader, I felt it my duty to return the discussion to her concern.

"You're already being divorced. Why would he want to kill you now?" I asked.

"For the most frequent motive: money. Behind a wall in the garage, I found financial files and offshore banking records. He's been hiding too much money to be gotten legally. A forensic accountant, testifying in open court, would bring the government down on him. He'd face prison time and the fear of his crooked partners that he'd turn on them in exchange for leniency. I threatened to expose him unless I'm given half. I supported his medical training and won't be cheated," she said firmly.

Chapter 88

Krystal's face showed more fear than fury but anger overcame her as she continued speaking.

"I'm a coffee addict. In the months before we separated, he'd insist on making coffee for me. He'd get up earlier and leave a thermos which I took to the office to drink throughout the day. I soon began having weird symptoms.

"My mouth felt dry and my breathing rate slowed with my chest feeling heavy. I developed pains in my joints and a burning in my vagina. I would feel nauseous but not vomit. My vision became blurred or distorted, and my ear canals felt tight and under pressure. I got headaches that lasted for days.

"I'd wake up at night with wet pajamas and then feel like I was freezing. I once lost consciousness and fell, needing stitches to my chin. There was also rectal bleeding. I can't begin to tell you how sick I felt. My doctors couldn't understand why I had these problems since my family was fine though we shared the same household."

"What did they conclude?" I asked.

"That my symptoms were idiopathic, meaning that they didn't know why particularly since my blood test results came back fine. I suffered until diagnosing the problem myself. My husband became furious when I'd forgotten to take the coffee he prepared. He described this as indicating his love for me but his over-the-top reaction planted a seed in my mind. All my symptoms disappeared when I stopped drinking the coffee that he made," Krystal said.

There was a group sigh. Krystal had described a wife's worst, almost indescribable fear.

"Did anything else suspicious happen?" Jenna asked.

After what she experienced, nothing criminal would surprise her.

"A gas leak was found in my office, two weeks after I told him I was filing for divorce," Krystal said.

Chapter 89

Krystal began sobbing.

"I loved him so much and had planned our life together. We would have three children and I'd be a typical soccer mom with a puppy and all. After the kids left for college, I'd maybe run for political office. I never wanted *this*," she said, contemptuously.

"No one does. We all have dreams until life gets in the way," Joanne said.

Needing a settling-down moment, I let the silence linger before returning to practicalities.

"It's easy to kill someone but not so easy to get away with it," I said.

Krystal pulled herself together and faced me.

"I need protection and don't know who to trust. I don't deal with criminal cases and am out of my element. You manage a security business. Do you handle these matters?" she asked.

"*Most* of our business is protecting ordinary people and diplomats. We can speak after the meeting."

I turned toward Sam.

"Can you stay for a few minutes afterward?" I asked.

"Sure," she said.

To our general relief, the remaining minutes involved other matters: recommendations of a hair-dresser, and problems with a child. Joanne's ten-year-old seemed a young version of Steve Jobs.

"Hopefully with a better personality. Put him near anything mechanical and he *must* figure out how it works. I tell him the possible danger but he needs a father," she said.

We turned away as she became teary.

The time for the group was over but none wanted to leave.

"Let's do something together, maybe go shopping," Jenna said.

I welcomed this suggestion and the others immediately agreed.

"How does Bergdorf-Goodman sound?" Erika asked.

That is her favorite store.

Chapter 90

While the others cleared the table of snacks and checked their makeup, I led Sam and Krystal to the bedroom used by Erika's father as an office. I spoke with each alone, feeling it best to discuss their issues privately in a more business-like setting.

The sleeping part of the room was curtained off by a sliding glass wall covered with floor-sweeping wool drapes. Beyond it was a library-office nook with red leather chairs, a banquette under a pendant lamp, and an ergonomic chair and desk with a printer on a table by its side. Throughout, greenery lay in pots of different size.

My talk with Sam was brief, just to gain enough information to have a company expert investigate her landlord, Anna. Sam provided her full name, her exact address, and her photo which had been taken during a party. Though Anna avoided having her picture taken, she had unsuspectingly appeared in the rear of a selfie that Sam took.

"These should be enough to identify her," I reassured Sam.

My talk with Krystal was more delicate. The most difficult topic for Americans to discuss is money. They're more open about their sex life, as evidenced by what celebrities freely reveal. Having gone from poverty to wealth in my life, I suffered with that hesitancy too.

Good personal security is costly. Most people can't afford it and I didn't know if Krystal could. She also had to learn why this is expensive.

"We provide good protection. Many of our clients are household names or diplomats. Our bodyguards have served

183

in the Special Forces of the United States, Britain, Germany, or Russia. We have never, I repeat, *never*, lost a client.

"Because our service is all-embracing, our prices range from three to five-thousand-dollars a day. Can you afford this?"

Obviously, I was a beginner at selling. A good salesperson doesn't start by describing their product's price as high.

To my surprise, Krystal didn't blink.

"When my husband learned that I found his records, he gave me an initial payment of two-million-dollars. I can afford it. How much is a life worth?" she asked.

What value indeed?

Chapter 91

There are two types of clothing shoppers: those who shop once a year and buy everything they might need and those like Erika who shop often. She is, as she has long described herself, "a *serious* shopper" who wants what she considers "the best." Billionaire's families can do this. Like I always say, their lives differ from your's and mine.

Bergdorf-Goodman is *her* store. Located on New York's Fifth Avenue opposite Central Park and the famed Plaza Hotel, it contains the newest fashions and a large restaurant to comfort the fashionable. I prefer smaller, more intimate settings but each to their own.

While Erika is perceptive, her judgment isn't perfect. Suggesting Bergdorf and its pricey restaurant for further bonding wasn't good. While money isn't her worry, it was for most of the others and passing unaffordable wares like Valentino Garavani's Pansy Bloom Leather Knee Boots costing nearly three-thousand dollars could arouse jealousy. Thus I shuffled us from the sales floors to the restaurant to outside as quickly as possible.

Erika grabbed the eatery's bill as soon as it arrived, commenting, "I have a store card." No one ever questioned her generosity.

Fortunately, this outing didn't damage the group's camaraderie and we hugged before going our separate ways.

While Jenna sat in front, chatting in Russian with the chauffeur, Erika and I sat in the rear. I was dozing when she spoke.

"Krystal's story is a frequent headline: *Man Kills Wife*."

"Domestic violence is a big risk in marriage. While expecting, I read that more deaths are caused by husbands than disease or infection during pregnancy," I said.

"That must have been reassuring," Erika said.

I couldn't help smiling.

"They usually kill themselves too," she said.

"Huh?"

"If the husband doesn't suicide, he often blames someone else for the crime after wounding himself to evidence his innocence."

"That wasn't in the article I read," I said.

It gave me something to think about as I drifted into sleep.

Chapter 92

Randy was waiting when I arrived home.

"How is your group going?" he asked.

"*Not* as I expected?" I said, slowly.

"How so?"

"I'm not sure and maybe because it isn't what I was looking for. I started the group right after giving birth and everything else that happened. I felt that I needed help, not exactly therapy but not so different from it either. I learned about support groups from accompanying a friend to one and thought that a group might be good for me too."

"You don't anymore?"

"I do and don't,"

"I'm confused."

"Join the club," I said.

After running his hand through his thick hair, he reached for me and I snuggled close.

"What's the matter, babe," he whispered.

"I feel like a rubber band that's been strung too often and near breaking. I should be strong," I said.

"You're the toughest person I know but everyone has their limit. Even titanium cracks at some point. Now I get it. You expected support from the group and aren't getting it," Randy said.

"It's not their fault. They simply have bigger problems than me. One woman fears that her landlord is a terrorist and another has a murderous husband. The others *are* dealing with my kind of stress but being the group leader I have to hold back,"

Silence followed. Our babies had been fed and would sleep for hours. Randy's hand began squeezing my groin rhythmically.

"Don't stop," I whispered.

Becoming parents had aged us but having sex on the rug made us feel young again.

"Promise me one thing," Randy said.

"What's that?"

"Well, I know how women like to shop so if you're ever with friends and there's a sale on the newest model vagina and all of them buy it, *you* won't! Your vagina is *perfect*, as tight as it was before," Randy said.

While that wasn't true, it was sweet of Randy to say it. Parenting had made him more sensitive. My phone's vibration brought the outside world crashing into ours.

Chapter 93

"I think I'm being followed," the voice said quickly.

"Huh?" I replied.

It took me a moment to recognize the voice.

"Krystal?"

"Yes."

"Where are you?"

"In the lobby of the Graybar Building on 42nd Street. I had a client meeting there," she said.

I thought for a moment.

"There's a passageway from the building into Grand Central Station. Police are always by the Information Booth. Stand near and keep your phone on. I'll have someone bring you in," I said.

"My daughter!"

"We'll get her too. Stay calm and don't leave Grand Central!" I ordered.

I hung up quickly to avoid wasting time with discussion.

"Trouble?" Randy asked.

"Business," I said, abruptly.

I was angry but not at him. Jordan had been hired for sales and not the operations role which I would now demand. I didn't think this would bother him but it would his wife. Fortunately, I'd placed his number in my speed-dial.

"We have an emergency. A new client believes someone is following her and we haven't yet assigned her protection. Have your pistol permits come through?" I asked.

"New York, New Jersey, and Connecticut, the other licenses too," he said.

"Good," I said.

I gave him Krystal's name, description, phone number, and location.

"Pick her up and then her child. Call me after you do that," I said.

"On my way," he said.

Jordan didn't waste words either.

Randy straightened his clothes.

"I'll stay with the kids while you deal with this," Randy said.

I only had time for a grateful smile. The company had safe houses in Europe but none in America. It was my job to create one but I hadn't done it. There are too many things to do, I told myself, pushing down my rising panic. Life was beginning to resemble high school.

Chapter 94

Being unsure how things would turn out, I sent Maria a text asking that she babysit that day. For use as a temporary safe house, I reserved two rooms at a local hotel: one for Krystal and her daughter and the other for their bodyguard.

I then remembered what else was needed: my apology to Elizabeth, Jordan's wife. She had expected his job to involve chatting-up clients and I had sent him on a protection assignment.

She picked up on the second ring.

"It's Margaret. I want to apologize for using Jordan on an operation. It's an emergency and I have no one else. He'll be home tonight and I'll try not to have it happen again," I said.

"Don't sweat it. Heb hates paperwork and was smiling as he ran out," she said.

"Heb? Are you Jewish?" I asked, being puzzled by the nickname.

"No, that's *Heeb*. If he were Jewish, he'd deck anyone who insulted him like that. Heb has been his nickname since West Point. It stands for Hard-Eyed Bastard," she said, with a laugh.

Feeling stupid, I changed the subject.

"How is your pregnancy coming?" I asked.

"Fine, except for not yet finding an obstetrician,"

"Let's get together and I'll tell you about mine. She's wonderful," I said.

"Great! Being alone is driving me crazy. I'm a compulsive worker and don't know how I'll stand the next six months."

"Come over tomorrow morning. I'll introduce you to my babies while they breakfast. Men don't make good pregnancy buddies," I said.

She laughingly agreed and I felt better after hanging up. Our conversation gave me an idea that could help us both.

Chapter 95

As it turned out, I didn't need Maria to babysit since my parents showed up without warning. Still, she always needed extra money and my babies loved her so I had her stay.

"Your father had rare free time so we thought to come over," my mother said.

"You're always welcome without an invitation. How is the life of a judge?" I asked, turning toward my father.

"Unlike a legal practice and with other worries," he said.

"How so?" I asked.

"Lawyers only defend clients and a jury renders the verdict. I must take that verdict to affect people's lives. It's a huge responsibility with constant uncertainties."

"Only a judge who feels that way merits the office. Moses told God that he wasn't up to his task too," my mother said.

"I'm no Moses even if people expect judges to be," my father said, with a smile.

"Well, I need a Moses so maybe God sent you here today," I said.

"What's the problem?" my father asked, in a serious tone.

"There's not yet a problem but I need advice to avoid one. I just hired an assistant, Jordan. He's a West Point graduate who left the Army at his wife's insistence. She's pregnant and wanted him home during her delivery which the service couldn't guarantee.

"She told me she's used to working and is going crazy staying home. I was thinking of hiring her part-time to help with office work and since she'll soon have an infant too, working together would be a joy. But I'm afraid that our friendship will clash with my being her husband's boss? What do you think?"

To my surprise, it was my mother who answered.

"I would consider it alright to be friendly but not intimate. Sharing parenting tips but not what goes on above her level of employment. You should also specify early on exactly what her tasks will be. If she's thoughtful, as I sense you consider her to be, there shouldn't be a problem," she said.

"I agree," my father said.

"Do you agree with mom about everything?" I asked, with a smile.

"Everything!" he said, firmly, not daring to risk a smile.

Chapter 96

Jordan phoned an hour later.

"Krystal's with me. We're going now to pick up her daughter," he said, quickly.

"Was there any problem?"

"None. Her tail was obvious and possibly intended to frighten her."

"OK. I've reserved two rooms at the Delamar Hotel on Greenwich Harbor. One for her and the other for her bodyguards who'll arrive shortly. Do you know where it is?" I asked.

"We spent a weekend there."

"Good. Call me if anything develops."

"Will do," Jordan said, and hung up.

I felt relieved though there was more to do. But for that, I needed Krystal's permission since the next step was confidential. She needed help that the company couldn't provide since her life was in legal jeopardy too.

One problem temporarily over. Now to deal with Sam's, I decided, and phoned Vladimir.

"She can't afford to hire us but helping her could be good for the company," I said.

I spoke hesitantly since only he could decide that.

"Tell me,"

"Samantha, a young member of my woman's group, fears that her roommate-landlord is a terrorist or spy. She's

195

older but parties with college kids, travels a lot, and avoids having her picture taken. She owns a pistol and studies improvised explosive devices.

"Sam doesn't want to lose her Manhattan room which is a great deal. I promised to have her landlord checked out," I said.

There was a momentary silence before Vladimir replied.

"That's easily done. If we find something, we'll tell the FBI and it'll give us more points with them. What facts do you have about the woman?"

"Her name, exact address, and a photo from Sam's selfie with her in the background. I'll send it all," I said.

"Good. Good thinking," Vladimir said, before hanging up.

We were too busy for family chit-chat.

Chapter 97

I waited for Jordan, Krystal, and her daughter, Kari, at the Delamar, checking their rooms and finding no failings. Nor did I expect since I had often stayed there with Randy before moving into my house. It had been *our* home away from our parents' homes.

I stood thinking on the suite's private balcony while watching the boats in the harbor. As I saw it, Krystal had three problems: to avoid indictment as an accessory to her husband's crimes; to keep her money though much derived from these crimes; and to remain safe despite her many enemies. Our company could only help with the last.

Did Krystal understand this? She would want to return to her customary life with Kari, working as a lawyer while her daughter attended her usual school. But this was over.

Upon their arrival, I showed them around the suite and asked if they had eaten. Eating reduces anxiety and I hoped it would have that effect here. I ordered from room service and described an excursion they might enjoy: a day trip to Greenwich's Island Beach which is a fifteen-minute ferry ride from the Hotel's backyard.

After eating, I left Kari to play Uno with Jordan in the living room while I had my heart-to-heart with Krystal in the bedroom.

"Jordan is a lovely man," she said.

"Yes, and happily married with a pregnant wife," I said, with an understanding smile.

"When will this be over? I don't begrudge the cost of your services but we have lives to live," Krystal said, calmly.

"You want to return home?" I asked.

"Maybe in a few days," she said, casually.

I let the silence build between us.

"Show me the files that you stole. I won't take notes but need to see them before assessing your risk and the services you'll need," I said.

"You won't try to copy them?"

"That's what I said."

Krystal opened her laptop and inserted a USB drive which she removed from her bra. She turned the screen toward me and I scanned the pages rapidly. When finished, I sighed, and turned toward Krystal.

"Your husband is clever," I said.

"Until I threatened him and everything blew up," she said.

Chapter 98

Krystal's husband hadn't only used his medical training conventionally.

"Do I get this straight? Together with accomplices, your husband sold drugs across the country by opening pharmacies which purchased large amounts of narcotics legally. Money was given to street people to fill prescriptions for phony ailments. After surrendering their drugs, they were given a place to stay until going out to make another drug purchase. The records refer to 'difficulties being taken care of' which I interpret as meaning a beating or murder," I said.

"That's how I interpreted it. So how soon can we go home?" Krystal repeated.

I winced before catching myself. Krystal wasn't stupid. She suffered from shock at the underpinnings of her life being torn away. This soccer mom was now running for her life and couldn't yet grasp it. Nor was she ready to listen.

I told her my assumptions, but slowly and carefully. To make them acceptable, I began with a story, as my lawyer-father often did with his clients before becoming a judge.

"Have you read Grisham's novel, *The Firm*?" I asked.

"No."

"It was a big seller and made into a movie. It's about a young lawyer in a situation like yours. The firm he joined turns out to be owned by the Mafia and if he tries to leave he'll be killed. When he does leave, the FBI and police want his head too. Safety seems impossible to achieve," I said.

The story engaged her interest. She was beginning to catch on.

"What does he do?"

"Just as you must do. With our help, you must be cleverer than those who would murder you," I said.

I spoke with greater assurance than I felt. That's what good sales people do.

Chapter 99

I had spoken in my role as company officer, believing that this would gain her greatest trust. It was not only me who could help her but the many who backed me.

"As we see it, you have both legal and security issues. Hopefully, a skillful lawyer will convince the government prosecutor that you're not your husband's accomplice. This can be done by providing them with the files you stole. Then your present life is over. Drug gangs are vicious, their memory is long, and they have great resources. You can never work as a lawyer again."

"That's no loss. I was starting to hate it," Krystal said.

"Good. You'll also need more money to live on for the rest of your life. Can you access your husband's bank accounts?" I asked.

"Yes. I stole the codes of his off-shore accounts too."

"Very good! Our company can't be involved but I'll teach you to open foreign accounts. Banks in Macao, Luxembourg, and Cyprus would be safest. After transferring his money into these, you'll be set for life.

"I suggest that you move to another English-speaking country. Your lawyer may be able to negotiate entry into Canada as a refugee. Canada has helped the American government in the past. Forty-years ago, the American hostages in Iran were rescued using authentic Canadian passports."

Krystal stared at me closely.

"You sound experienced," she said.

"I've led a colorful life," I said.

"I'm ready for a drab one."

"That's our goal, for you and your daughter."

We got busy. From our files, I provided Krystal with contacts at three banks that our company had done business with. Within two hours, she gained the required identification PINs and sequential clearing codes for online transactions. Seventy-four-million dollars was transferred from her husband's off-shore accounts into her's.

"That will keep you comfortable and pay for your daughter's education. Did you leave your husband anything?" I asked.

"Enough so he won't wind up on the street," Krystal said, in a voice as hard as flint.

She went to retrieve her daughter from the adjoining room.

Chapter 100

I left Krystal with Jordan and returned home. There, I greeted Maria, fed my babies, and went to my home-office to phone my father,

"The Judge is in court," his secretary informed me.

"Please ask him to call his daughter, Margaret, when he's free. I need his advice but also tell him that everything is fine," I said.

Parents worry when receiving unexpected phone calls from their children.

While waiting, I turned to a parenting book that I had been reading, stopping at the chapter on teenagers. I didn't want to become more a worrier than I was.

"What's up, dear?" my father asked, just as I'd put down the book.

"I need the name of a good lawyer," I said.

"Are you in trouble?" he asked, in a tone that suddenly turned serious.

"No, it's for a client. She needs a lawyer to negotiate with the Justice Department. Though not a criminal, she's willing to provide evidence of a nationwide drug trafficking enterprise in exchange for immunity from prosecution and new identities for her and her daughter," I said.

"A good lawyer is expensive."

"She can afford it."

"D. D. Palmer would be best even if he is a bit odd," my father said, after some thought.

"How so?" I asked.

"As a teenager, he grew marijuana in his father's garden and was arrested for urinating his name into wet concrete. Later, he wore psychedelic neckties, fluorescent shoelaces, and clothes with colors from a lollypop jar. I haven't seen him in years though he lives locally."

"No prosecutor could resist him," I said, with a laugh.

"Possibly not. Before entering practice, he was the U.S. Attorney for the Southern District of New York."

Mr. Palmer picked up on the third ring. My father's description of him impressed me for to have behaved so individually required self-assurance. After introducing myself, I told him who referred me and why I called.

"An endangered lawyer. It sounds like a novel," he said.

"Her situation is desperate. Are you available?" I said.

"I'm semi-retired but the case would make a change from babysitting grandchildren," he said.

"That's great! Give me your address and we'll be right over. What is your fee?" I asked.

"Five-hundred-dollars an hour and a ten-thousand-dollar initial retainer," he said.

"The money will be wired to you today," I promised.

In the background, I heard a child scream, "Grandpa," as we hung up.

Chapter 101

I told Maria that I would return in several hours and went to pick up Krystal. Once back with her daughter, she looked calmer and welcomed my news.

"Your daughter can come with us. She can play with his grandchildren while we talk," I said.

I turned toward Jordan,

"I expect the bodyguards to arrive from Germany within a few hours. You'll be home late tonight," I promised.

"No sweat. I haven't had this much fun in years," he said, with a smile.

Palmer's house was a large colonial two miles outside Greenwich. The door was opened by his wife, a tall, casually dressed woman in her fifties. She coaxed Krystal's daughter away and led us toward her husband's home-office. We refused her offer of coffee.

Palmer's clothes weren't as my father had described. Doubtless, those flamboyant days had long been over. Now, he wore the three-piece suit typical of pricey lawyers. Only the red-green-blue necktie hinted at his colorful past.

Krystal briefly described her problems.

"I've had two attempts on my life after telling my husband that I was divorcing him. He obviously fears his finances being revealed in court and wants to stop this. By snooping, I've discovered his involvement in a criminal drug operation that spans America and reaches into Canada.

"Since we're an affluent couple, I want to prevent the government from charging me with criminal involvement and to ignore the money which I've taken from his accounts. I'm in hiding and can never work again. I need a good lawyer and was told that you're the best," Krystal said.

"Flattery will get you anything with me," Palmer said, with a smile.

He turned toward Jordan.

"You are?" he asked.

"Her bodyguard," he said.

"Of course."

The silence grew heavy as Palmer doodled on a pad. Finally, he spoke.

"I'll accept your case but the others must leave for our discussion to retain the lawyer-client privacy privilege. They can wait in the library, down the hall on the right."

Krystal's meeting took nearly an hour. While waiting, I scanned the books on the shelves, settling for a large pictorial atlas of New York City in the nineteen-forties. Jordan sprawled in a chair and tried to nap.

Krystal was smiling when she entered the room. Her look was the best news that I had all day.

Chapter 102

Only the waiting remained, for the legal wrangling with the government to end. But I couldn't leave things as they were. Krystal and Kari had to be kept calm while their fate was being decided. Hiding friendless in a hotel, even one as comfortable as the Delamar, wasn't an enviable life. Any stranger could be a threat, and she had business obligations. Her law partners must learn that she would not be returning and her clients would have to be reassigned. Though painful, her safety came first.

Kari had adjustments to make too. She couldn't be trusted with online media or have contact with her father. When I questioned this effect on her development, Krystal denied it.

"He never wanted children and I was pretty much a single parent. He's not in any of the photos that I took of her achievements. She calls him her 'travel daddy,'" Krystal said.

"She'll have a lifetime to work it out," I said, supportively.

"I hope to get her a better substitute," Krystal said.

Having moved on emotionally, she was already considering her husband's replacement and eyed her bodyguards speculatively.

Jason was a six-foot three-inch, thirty-nine-year-old man of evident physical strength. Though speaking little, he was shrewd and possessed excellent judgment. He had been a professional soldier in Britain's counter-terrorism unit, the Special Air Service (SAS).

Earl was a compact man of five-foot ten-inches and four years older. He still had the build of the boxer he had earlier been. He was reported to have nerves of steel and be efficient with all weapons.

Jason had an air of authority. Earl let him do the talking which consisted of passing on basic security tradecraft. While I played Uno with Kari, Krystal listened attentively. Jason's lesson could save their lives.

Chapter 103

Jason was a good teacher. After handing Krystal an instruction sheet, he went over it point-by-point. I listened while playing cards. The game required little concentration particularly since Kari played by her own rules. "I'm a great player," she said, and I wasn't brave enough to disagree.

"Forget the James Bond antics. Avoiding threat is your best defense since you then won't be risking your life. Many people are superstitious, believing that if they don't think about danger it won't happen. But danger *does* happen so you must be continually alert.

"You must estimate the risk of each new situation, leaving quickly if it seems dangerous. After a while, this habit becomes second nature and provides you with a good deal of safety.

"Another danger is the fear of humiliation, being so concerned with avoiding embarrassment that you won't call loudly for help or flee. Like not leaving a self-service elevator if a drunken hulk enters.

"After moving to a new city, it'll take time to learn the dangerous areas so try to stay with relatives or a trust-worthy friend until you decide where to settle. Investigate the neighborhood before committing yourself.

"Once you decide on a building, immediately change the locks. If the landlord insists on having the new keys in case of emergency, provide them in a sealed envelope so you'll know if anyone entered in your absence. Losing your keys can lead to a burglary or worse. Don't put Ms. or Mrs. on your mailbox. Instead, use your initial like J. Jones. Then, a potential burglar won't know if you're a police officer or weightlifter.

"If your building has a self-service elevator and you enter at the ground floor, place your foot in the door and leave at once if the basement indicator is lit. Someone may be waiting there, using the elevator to bring you to him.

"Now it's story time, to learn how we saved our lives so you'll feel confident that we can protect you."

Chapter 104

"When in a tight spot it's critical to keep focused on your mission. You tell yourself you're immortal and joke that dying doesn't bother you but you don't want to be there when it happens.

"We didn't want to be there that night. The risk was so high that we carried *two* death pills in case we weren't getting out and couldn't shoot ourselves after running out of ammunition. Being burned alive in a cage online wasn't our favored goodbye to relatives," Jason said.

Our eyes bored into his. He had captured our attention. I was glad that Kari was focused on our game and not listening. Her skillful cheating required concentration.

"The target for exfiltration, removing from danger, was an ISIS technical expert. He saw no future in radicalism and wanted out. He'd contacted an embassy official and, after negotiation, accepted our offer: relocation to the West for he and his wife; new identity and citizenship for both, and a ten-million-dollar payment. This was high but his information was priceless: the financial records of all illegal oil shipments from the so-called Caliphate and the locations of its leaders. Killing them with drones would save many lives, civilian and military.

"We arrived for our meeting and waited. He arrived late, sweating and nervous, wearing a thick jacket though the coolness of the evening hadn't set in. Feeling uneasy but reluctant to abort, I ordered him to stay thirty feet away as we spoke. When I asked where his suitcase and wife were, he said he decided to leave everything and that his wife would meet him later. This didn't make sense and my unease increased.

"When he moved closer, gunfire erupted toward us and the blast from his explosive vest knocked us down. Either his defection had been discovered or it had always been a scam, possibly with his wife's safety being used as incentive for cooperating.

"The look-down, missile-firing drone which I had earlier ordered saved us. Protecting you couldn't present greater danger," Jason said.

Krystal gripped Jason's arm as she spoke confidently.

"We'll need luck to survive and you've got it," she said.

Chapter 105

Jason ended his lecture, feeling that was enough instruction for one day. "A little at a time is best," he said.

Keeping Krystal's family safe was my duty but so was the welfare of mine. Despite my worry, James and Donna were enjoyably playing with Maria when I arrived home. I pushed down my resentment at not being missed. They would be hungry soon.

I was writing notes of the day's activity when Erika arrived. Her bodyguard, Abram, carried a large carton.

"Your babies need transportation," she said, opening it.

The carton contained a Thule Chariot Cross stroller.

"It'll carry both. You can take them skiing using its attachment," Erika said.

"I don't ski," I said, grumpily.

"Wow! You're in some mood."

"I'm sorry, it's the job. I thought it would just be assigning bodyguards and doing paperwork. Being responsible for people's safety reduces their worry but adds to mine. A mistake could mean their life," I said.

"That's what police officers face every day. It's good you're doing it and not someone who doesn't worry. How is Krystal getting along?" Erika asked.

"As good as can be expected. She and her bodyguards mesh well but sitting around doing nothing will drive her crazy and she has no friends here. She needs to get her mind off her troubles while her lawyer does his thing," I said.

"You can't beat the security at my home. Why not invite her to a party there?" Erika asked.

"Who would come?" I asked, slowly.

"Our families, my dad's business associates, and the babies of course. My step-mom is pregnant," Erika said.

"*She's pregnant*?" I questioned, with surprise.

"Sara isn't *that* old and my dad is proud as can be. It's been a long time since he played with a baby. Being with your's could help re-acquaint him."

Chapter 106

Krystal loved Erika's idea of a party. She had been at loose ends after resigning from her law firm. Though technically still both a lawyer and a wife, these roles were now gone. She said sorrowfully, "It would be a lie to say I'm his wife. I both love and hate him."

Erika's parties are never simple affairs. Creating them had been her forte since high school and she throws herself into it. Just having favors for kids and small talk for adults isn't her style.

"I could make it like Vegas," she mused.

"*Oh no*," I burst out.

"*What*?" Krystal asked.

"Tell her," I said, and Erika did.

"My dad was invited to a bash in Las Vegas. Sara wasn't in the mood to go because of morning sickness and her kids weren't available but I was. He wouldn't have gone if he'd known what it would be like. It isn't his scene," Erika said.

"How so?" Krystal asked.

"It was the ultimate birthday party for a billionaire, at a hotel suite costing thirty-thousand-dollars a night. It had a pool on its terrace overlooking the Strip, a Ferris wheel, a cigar lounge, and a trampoline. Besides bankers, the other guests were from Hollywood and TV. We stayed only a few minutes before going downstairs where I won a hundred-dollars in the slots. We flew back next morning."

"*That* won't be your party?" Krystal asked, with mock disappointment.

Margaret: Mother of Twins

"Hardly, but I'll do my best," Erika said, with a laugh.

I didn't worry. Even Erika's worst is always great.

Chapter 107

"It isn't easy," Erika complained, the next morning.

She had taken to visiting me often, chuckling to one child while I fed the other. Gaining tips and experience for her future as a mother.

"What isn't?" I asked, more tightly grasping the fidgeting James.

"Creating a party for guests ranging from excited infants to respite-needing parents," Erika said.

"You can do it if anyone can," I said, supportively.

And she did. Erika divided her home's basement recreation room into three sections: one for toddlers and young children complete with well-credentialed babysitters; one for adults to mingle; and a third for teenagers to do the same. While each section had the right foods and drinks, I felt that renting arcade–style slot machines for the teenagers was a bit much. Each was given four rolls of quarters to play with.

Easily walked-around screens provided a sense of privacy for the teenagers but the ability of parents to check on them too, making for a reassuring setting.

The guests were: the families of previously-vetted business associates of Erika's father; my parents and sisters; Erika's step-mother and her adult children; my brother and his girlfriend, Kimberly, and her young daughter; and my friend from Barnard, Missy, who brought her husband and her toddler, Cordelia.

The adult talk was hushed, the teenagers weren't too boisterous, and the younger ones were a pleasure. To maintain her security, I introduced Krystal as Abby, a

Greenwich resident newly arrived from Boston. My father gave me a knowing look but said nothing.

Erika's father wowed the adults with stories of his business coups and my father captured attention with his legal stories.

I watched Krystal socialize. She mostly listened, only occasionally adding a brief remark. She looked relaxed which was the purpose of the party. But it also gave others the chance to ventilate.

Kimberly, a native of Brazil and billionaire heiress, was distressed by the recent fire at Brazil's National Museum in Rio de Janeiro.

"It held specimens ranging from dinosaur fossils to artifacts of vanished Amazon tribes. I've been to the Louvre in Paris but like most Brazilians had never been to ours. Brazil sees itself as a country of the future but will never achieve this without knowing its history," she moaned.

When a friend is sad, sometimes all they need is a silent listener. We stood apart in our own world until a robotic female voice startled everyone and ended the party: "There has been a security breach. Go to your assigned secure location." Moments later, heavily armed bodyguards stormed into the room and led us to an underground chamber.

Chapter 108

Erika's boast that her home's security equals that of the White House isn't empty. Each floor has a steel-lined security room containing porta-potties, food, guns, and an independent telephone line and auxiliary air supply.

While a past houseguest, I had suffered alerts in a smaller security room. This one was much the same. Then, it held me, Erika, and our boyfriends. Here, were many more accompanied by three bodyguards.

Ten minutes later, the all-clear sounded and we joked to relieve tension. Two teenagers, seeking their crashed drone, had innocently trespassed onto the estate only to be restrained by armed, foreign-accented guards. They were quickly released with their drone and the incident gave the now calm party guests an oft-repeated story. "Better safe than sorry," was the voiced sentiment as they hurriedly left.

"Once a party goes flat, it's hard to reawaken it," Erika said.

Missy remained. Much had happened since we spoke many months before. I had given birth and her daughter and marriage were older. Cordelia played a board game with her step-father in a far corner of the room, gorging on the remained cupcakes.

"Being married is fun but takes effort," Missy said, watching them carefully.

I listened closely, hoping to achieve that "fun" one day.

"How so?" I asked.

"Continuing upkeep is needed with the woman doing most of it. I accept that Cordelia is *my* child and he's great with her when he's around, but..."

"Medical school is hard," I said.

"There's the in-law problem too," Missy said.

Family is important to Russians and her husband's father was a Russian diplomat. Missy wanted the family to remain in America despite pressure to settle in Moscow.

"You can work it through," I said supportively.

"I won again!" Cordelia screamed with delight.

"She cheats," Missy said, with a smile.

Chapter 109

"All-in-all, you *could* call the party a success," Erika said, after the last guest left.

"Sure," I said, disinterestedly.

"It wasn't *that* bad."

"That's not what's depressing me. It's that my group isn't working as planned. Enid and Krystal are gone and Sam may be leaving soon. The group has a higher death rate than an oil rig," I said.

"*They're not dead*," Erika said, with a laugh.

"Yes, but they are gone. I'll have to give a convincing reason or end the group which I'd hate doing. They're good people and I feel that I'm gaining from being with them though not sure how," I said.

"Helping others with their difficulties lessens a person's worrying," Erika said.

"OK, but doesn't anyone have *normal* problems? Those without a Mafia boyfriend or murdering husband or terrorist roommate."

"They were a bit unusual," Erika said.

"You do tend toward understatement," I said, glumly.

We both laughed and Erika became serious.

"Joanne and Vera are dealing with widowhood and Jenna needs all the help she can get," she said.

"I'll keep the group going until we all graduate from it," I said, in a determined tone.

"With a diploma?"

"And a party but certainly not at your house," I said, feeling upbeat again.

The following Saturday, my optimism continued as I explained Krystal's absence to the group.

"She's decided to start over, far away," I said.

Long before, I had learned that it's best to keep a lie close to the truth.

"She's smart, and a lawyer can get a job anywhere. Having only one child makes it easier too," Vera said.

She had no children. Joanne, who spoke next, had three at home.

"My husband died months ago but some everyday things are still painful. This turkey sandwich reminds me of him. He loved them and I loved fixing them for him," she said.

Her earnest tone begged us to understand.

Chapter 110

For Joanne, the turkey sandwich had been a reminder of what she lost. But what of her future and that of her children? Which was what I said.

"You seem to have lost touch with your future and that of your children," I said, softly.

I thought of asking if she had begun dating before deciding that this question would be too intrusive. That Jenna didn't think this surprised me. Considering her having been raped, I believed that men would be the last thing on her mind.

"Are you dating anyone seriously?" Jenna asked.

"I'm not sure," Joanne replied.

Her response didn't make sense and we awaited an explanation.

"I was sent to a Manhattan workshop along with a guy from the New Haven office. After class, we had dinner at the hotel and one thing led to another.

"He's eight years older and has two teenagers. His wife died of cervical cancer last year and we were each other's first date since... The conference lasted four days and we were together each night so I guess we're dating but it's been three days since and he hasn't called me. He's a bit shy so maybe he's waiting for me to call. I don't know."

"What did he say when you last spoke?" I asked.

"He said he'd call. We couldn't kiss, others were around."

"Do you want to see him again?" Jenna asked.

"We're in the same situation and do the same work," Joanne said.

"We get that it's a match. Do you *really* like him. How are you two in bed?" Jenna asked.

Joanne's face colored and it was several moments before she answered.

"The sex was the best that I ever had and he said the same. He's the first lover to match my interest in sex and we studied it together. My mind is stuck with him but I feel guilty too, like I've betrayed my husband."

Indecision tore at her face.

"Go for it. Call him! What can you lose?" Jenna advised.

"*I will,*" Joanne said resolutely, after a fleeting silence.

Feeling pleased, I looked at the others. They looked happy too.

Chapter 111

I was smiling broadly upon my return home.

"What is it?" Randy asked.

"The group is going well. We helped a member make an important decision," I said.

"About a man?"

"Yes."

Sensing that I wasn't about to share more, Randy changed the subject.

"We have decisions to make too," he said.

Anxiety flooded through me and my heart skipped a beat. It is the feeling that every single women gets when their boyfriend suddenly adopts a serious tone. Is he about to say "it's over" with "it's not working" or "you deserve someone better" coming next, she asks herself. This, even if there isn't and never would be.

"I've been accepted into Columbia's Ph.D. program with free tuition and a teaching assistant job. They're excited about some software that I'm working on and say it'll make a great dissertation. There's talk of starting a company to market the rights. With luck I could graduate in three years."

"That's wonderful! What's the problem?" I asked.

I felt relief that Randy hadn't voiced my fear. But did it come from what I sensed about our relationship or the anxiety that every single mother feels when their children's father has the option of leaving for a less taxing life? I pushed down these thoughts.

"You wanted to move to Utah when I finish college," Randy said.

"That was a fantasy, when we weren't sure how our lives would develop. Now with the babies and my office in Greenwich, settling here would be perfect. Living in Manhattan would also be fine if that's what you want," I said.

"It's what you want too. We're a team," he said.

"We are."

I moved us to face the full-length mirror.

"Aren't we a handsome couple?" I asked, rhetorically.

"And make beautiful babies," Randy said.

Though kissing me, he didn't say what I hoped: that we needed to set a wedding date.

Chapter 112

Erika had been having what looked like a serious conversation with Maria when I entered the room. Though curious, I didn't ask what it concerned. I would learn soon enough if either wanted me to know. I did learn while breastfeeding Donna as Maria held James.

"Erika is *awfully* smart," Maria said.

"She is."

"She never treats me rudely because I'm poor. Not like some do."

"I can empathize since my family was once poor. Erika is a gem. Being wealthy has never made a difference in how she treats others and she's the most generous person I know," I said.

"She told me that the signs of decent breeding are alertness, having a good sense of humor, good character, and considering good looks as insignificant. That's brilliant!" Maria said.

"She's also brilliant," I agreed, smiling as I exchanged babies with her.

The house phone rang and, while carrying Donna, Maria went to answer it.

"It's for you, a woman called Abby," she said.

It was Krystal, using the false name that I assigned her for Erika's party.

"What's doing?" I asked, moving the squirming James to a more comfortable position.

"I have a problem. We must talk," Krystal said, abruptly.

"The kids are feeding. Can you come over?" I asked.

"I'm on my way."

Krystal arrived with her two bodyguards and daughter. While we spoke, Kari and my babies entertained one other.

"What's on your mind?" I asked.

"My lawyer called. Negotiations with the Justice Department are progressing. They're no longer making an issue about money but insist that I take a lie detector test to be sure I wasn't criminally involved."

"*OK*," I said slowly.

Her voice had become increasingly hysterical. To calm her, I spoke in a measured tone.

"There's a difference between a small problem and a life-threatening situation. What's your fear?" I asked.

Chapter 113

"What do you know about the polygraph?" Krystal asked.

"Just a little. A company director is a retired CIA official. He's spoken about Rick Ames, a Russia spy. Ames beat his polygraph test twice so it's not infallible. But don't try to as by holding your breath since this'll indicate that you're lying. What's your worry?" I asked.

"What will they ask?"

"Again, I'm no authority so I only know what was told me. The examiner first gets a baseline of your physiological responses by asking what they already know. Things like your date of birth and where you went to school. They then focus on what they want to learn. With you it'll probably be when you first learned of your husband's crimes and possible involvement."

"Will they ask about sex?" Krystal asked, in a nervous tone.

"I can't see how that might be relevant. Maybe with someone who could be blackmailed if the sex was truly off-beat but they wouldn't care whatever you do. Your lawyer said their only interest is if you were your husband's accomplice so..."

"Oh. How can I be sure to pass?" Krystal asked.

"You can't. Again, I can only repeat what I was told. The best preparation is to get a good night's sleep and think calm thoughts. You were almost killed twice and had nothing to do with the drug business. Why are you worried?" I asked.

There was silence while Krystal considered how much to reveal. *Was* she innocent? I asked myself.

"What do you think about Kira?" Krystal asked.

"Why do you ask? She's a delight."

"Yes, but does she resemble *me*?" Krystal asked.

"Not at all. You're Mediterranean and she's a Nordic blond with blue-eyes and angular features. She looks like her father," I said.

"She does. Her real father," Krystal replied.

I understood.

Chapter 114

"Does your husband know he's not Kari's father?" I asked.

"I sense that he always suspected it. We rarely had sex about the time I conceived. I met Kari's father at a restaurant and things went from there. He was a single Danish diplomat who gets re-assigned every four years. His next post was in Riyadh and I couldn't see living there or regularly changing countries. My husband's suspicion may be why he's never been a father to Kari but he also can't relate to kids," Krystal replied.

"Stop worrying! Adultery isn't criminal and you should easily pass the polygraph. Since there's no evidence connecting you to any crime, so as long as you don't confess to something the government has nothing," I said.

"You're probably right. It's nerves," Krystal said.

"When is your exam?"

"Tomorrow morning, at the FBI headquarters in Manhattan."

"I'll babysit Kari. If something comes up, my mother or Maria can pitch in," I said.

"Your company provides good service," Krystal said, with her first smile that day.

"We aim to please. Think good thoughts!" I repeated.

One crisis down, I thought, as I joined the baby-induced melee with the others. My bliss vanished when I picked the local newspaper off the floor and saw a headline: "Religious Leader Hospitalized After Heroic Rescue of Child."

Margaret: Mother of Twins

Mother Marie, an esteemed religious figure and my adviser for years, had saved a child's life by pushing him from the path of a drunken driver. She lay hospitalized in "serious condition." At eighty-seven-years of age, a patient's "serious condition" meant perilous.

Chapter 115

The Yoruba people migrated from Egypt to the Nigerian region of Africa between 2000 B.C. and 500 B.C. Led by their King Oduduwa, they established their sacred capital of Ile-Ifa with Oyo as its governmental seat.

Around 1400 A.D., Yoruba armies created an empire which was later destroyed by European slave traders and Islamic Holy Warriors. Many slaves who were transported to the New World came from the Yoruba elite of soldiers and warrior-priests. Here, their persecuted religion survived by going underground, hiding its traditional beliefs and practices alongside the dominant religion of Christianity.

In the European colonies, the Yoruba religion had different names: Lucumi in Cuba, Voodun in Haiti, Condomble in Brazil, and Santeria in Puerto Rico. Mother Marie is an Iyalorisha (priestess) of Santeria.

As a child, I suffered from a genetic deformity, Sanfilippo disease. This, it was predicted, would eventually kill me for I lacked the essential enzyme enabling cells to properly break down sugars. The famed Johns Hopkins Medical Center had given my parents no hope.

Learning of my condition, Mother Marie, who had been tutoring my sister in French, after consulting the Gods in prayer, advised my parents to add soybeans to my diet. This miraculously healed me and, after research, became the standard medical treatment for Sanfilippo disease.

Though considered peculiar, noted American personalities have followed the Santeria religion. Among them is the co-star of the enormously popular 1950s TV sit-com, *I Love Lucy*, which can still be seen in reruns. When Desi

Arnaz sang, "Babalu, Babalu, Babalu Aye, Babalu Aye," he was invoking one of the most powerful Yoruba Gods, Babaluaye, the healer of sickness and epidemics. Following my recovery, I chose Him as my spiritual husband.

After divining my future through Yoruba ritual, Mother Marie had guided my life onto its destined path. Our prayers gained me protection from the Gods and saved my life. I would go to the hospital to pray for hers.

Chapter 116

Before leaving for the hospital, I dressed soberly as one does for church. If Mother Marie was able, we could pray for her recovery together. Otherwise, I would pray alone.

The waiting room was over-flowing when I arrived. Mother Marie's counsel had helped many people and all seemed to have come. Her son, a hedge fund manager, greeted me warmly when I arrived. I had often been to her apartment which is in the same condominium as my biological mother's.

"How is she?" I asked, with eyes that begged for good news.

"The doctor said her condition is still serious," he said.

"Can she have visitors?" I asked.

"She's sedated now but possibly tomorrow."

I spoke in the ancient tongue.

"*B'ao ku ishe o tan. Ise Olorun tobi. Mo fe bo.*" (When there is life, there is still hope. God's work is great and mighty. I want to worship.)

He led me to the interdenominational chapel where we kneeled, I prayed to Orunmila who, when living, was the prophet of the Yoruba religion. As a divinity, he was present when humans were created and knows their destiny. In the Yoruba religion, he is comparable to the "son of God." Though crippled and born of poor West African parents, his wisdom was recognized early and he grew to be known as "the little man with the big head."

While capable of action and speech, Orunmila has no physical form and no sculptures of him exist. He is present through the divinatory rites performed by priests. I prayed

"Orunmila, witness of fate, thou are more effective than medicine.

"Thou art the immense orbit that averts the day of death, to thee salutation is first due in the morning.

"Thou are the equilibrium that adjust world forces and the repairer of misfortune. Those who know thee become immortal."

Soon after closing my eyes, I felt myself in endless space, traveling through a tunnel drilled in time. Far down the black and grey dimness, I saw the light of sunrise. A voice came from a cloud, thundering like wind exiting a tunnel: "*Aye l'oja, orun n'ile. Dide died lalafia.*" (The world is a marketplace. The spirit world is home. Arise, arise in peace.)

We rose and left the chapel. We could do no more. Medical care and the Gods would determine Mother Marie's fate.

Chapter 117

Mother Marie rallied though whether because of prayer or medicine no one cared. Her vital signs improved rapidly and, almost miraculously, she returned home three days later. This time she accepted her son's offer to hire a helper with her chores. "Age produces limits," he insisted, a position which cannot reasonably be argued.

I visited her as soon as became possible. First at the hospital and later at her apartment. Despite my Mormon upbringing, I brought James and Donna to the later visits, knowing that their presence would raise her spirits but also to seek their blessing. "The Gods are not jealous," she had often said, and one could not have too many blessings.

My babies weren't unaware of their new surroundings. After moments of quiet, they related to Mother Marie in a manner unlike their usual selves. If not with reverence then certainly with interest, listening to her words and being calmed by their tone.

I brought Mother Marie up-to-date on my hectic life. She listened attentively, saying little. Idle chatter is not her manner. Finally, she spoke.

"The Gods have favored you and you have become wise beyond your years. I will tell you a story, how the crocodile became powerful with the aid of Elegguá. You know of Him?"

"He is one of the most important Gods, beyond good and evil. He is justice personified, punishing or rewarding with perfect equanimity. Helping if one behaves correctly and creating havoc if one behaves improperly, knowing things that no one else knows," I said.

"Yes. The crocodile was once the largest and most graceful creature in the river. His soft skin was deep brown and he swam smoothly. But his beauty brought envy from the fish and frogs with whom he shared the river. They ganged up on him and he feared them.

"'You are so big. Why do you tolerate them?' asked Elegguá.

"'Because the frogs make terrible noises which disturb my sleep and the fish bite me with their sharp teeth when my back is turned.'

"'You need to make *ebo* (sacrifice to the Gods), Bring me twenty-one coconuts and twenty-one iron spikes and you'll never be afraid again,' Elegguá advised.

"The crocodile had never heard of *ebo* but he trusted Elegguá and did as he was told. The next morning, Elegguá placed the spikes in his gums, giving him sharp teeth. Then he split the coconuts and put the shards down his spine and sides. 'Now you need not fear anything,' he said.

"Since then, the crocodile has been the most powerful creature on the river with teeth so sharp that he can eat anything and a skin so hard that no one can hurt him," Mother Marie said.

I immediately grasped her lesson and spoke.

"*Ojo o buru, ebon ii gbe ni o.*" (In days of turbulence, it is ebo that saves.)

I looked at my babies. They slept peacefully beside Mother Marie.

Chapter 118

The following weeks passed unequally. My babies thrived as did my family. My father's career as a judge went well and his demeanor and decisions attracted favorable comment.

Randy accepted the offer of doctoral study at Columbia University's Department of Computer Science but we had not yet decided where to live. While his commute from Greenwich to Columbia's Manhattan campus was workable, living in the City would be easiest for him. But the many captivating women in Manhattan continued my fear for our relationship even as business concerns remained.

The Justice Department's negotiations about Krystal's future proved tough and Sam's worry about her landlord continued. But our group was now out of these issues and helped with common difficulties: mine, Jenna's, Vera's, and Joanne's.

The departures of Krystal and Enid left marks. We had become close and their absence hurt. There was no way to avoid this, which was what I said.

"I also miss them and wish that their leaving had been more formal, like sharing their future plans at a going-away party. But life isn't like that. Unlike men, women do cry when they like someone so tears are OK. Success and fun go hand-in-hand so we'll have faith that's what they're experiencing. Now, who's next?" I asked, with an expectant look.

All eyes turned toward Joanne.

"*What*?" she asked, with a smile.

"Did you call him?" Vera asked.

"Yes, and he said that he'd hungered to see me but his son fractured a bone in his foot while skateboarding and he'd been busy with medical appointments and work deadlines. It's too early in the relationship for our kids to meet. We couldn't stay over either's place and rented a room at the Marriott for the day. Officially, we were working from home," Joanne said.

"But you *did* speak about work matters," Vera said, in a mock serious tone.

"Absolutely! For a moment as we entered the hotel," Joanne replied, with a grin.

Chapter 119

Krystal phoned soon after I arrived home. She wanted to meet and I invited her and her daughter for dinner. They and their bodyguards arrived promptly at six. My babies, dozing after dining, soon fell asleep. This disappointed Kari who expected to play with them.

I eased her disappointment with a visit to their bedroom and the gift of an Operation board game. In it, body parts must be gingerly removed lest a buzzer sound and a red bulb light. Kids love it despite its unpleasant undertone. As Krystal's bodyguards relaxed with coffee and cookies in the library, she told me the latest.

"All but the paperwork is over. I passed the polygraph test and will be granted immunity from prosecution. We could enter the Witness Protection Program with new identities or go on our own. I chose to go with them," Krystal said.

"I think you made the right decision," I said.

"Yes, though they might be glad to be rid of us. I didn't know how long we'd be here so I began enrolling Kari in a small private school. She needed a measles vaccination and while an FBI man drove us there, she threw up in the back seat."

"*Oh, God,*" I said, stifling a laugh.

"Yes, but the agent was nice. 'It's a government car and needed cleaning,' he said, calmly."

"When will you be leaving?" I asked.

"Soon. The paperwork should be finished a few weeks. Then I give them the files and it'll be over."

"Don't tell me but do you know where you'll be going?"

"I haven't decided or what to do. I was happiest being a working mom and aren't looking forward to staying home. But working as a lawyer would make me a public figure and be too risky," Krystal said.

"Maybe you could do volunteer legal consulting for a government agency," I said.

"It's an idea but government bureaucracy doesn't do well with volunteers," Krystal said.

"You might be lucky. Luck happens when opportunity meets preparation. Be prepared!" I said, in a fake commanding tone.

"I am. I'm searching for my grown-up Boy Scout," Krystal said, with a smile.

Chapter 120

The drizzly weather over the next week colored the moods in my home. My babies fretted and Maria was preoccupied. Even my family's bodyguard, Mila, who would often raise my spirits, shared the household depression.

"What's wrong?" I finally asked her.

"Living alone gets to one," Mila said.

"When was your last date?" I asked.

"I barely remember."

"I don't get it. You're smart and beautiful. What's *wrong* with the men here?"

"*What's wrong* is that Greenwich is a family town with virtually no single men in their thirties. Men in their twenties can Tinder-swipe dates but I'm too old for that and have a lousy background too."

"Nonsense! Having been a doctor and a police officer and a soldier makes you fascinating," I insisted.

"It scares men off. They don't want a professional woman who can wrestle them to the ground. They want a smiling adorer with big breasts," Mila said.

"You have those too," I said.

"Well, the boobs," she admitted.

"Erika helps her father and knows many executives. Maybe she can find you a guy."

Mila gave me a look.

"I'm *serious*. Vladimir wants our bodyguards radiating calm. Not looking like bouncers readying for a take-down. It gives us a crummy reputation," I said.

"Do I look that bad?"

"I exaggerated but will talk to Erika," I said.

I did and her instant solution was unexpected.

"I *do* know someone. He's a thirty-six year old, newly-arrived scientist, divorced and desperately lonely according to my dad. I'll invite both for a weekend and put them in adjoining rooms. That should do it," Erika said.

"If not, they belong back in high school," I said.

"I wouldn't wish that on anyone," Erika said, with a laugh.

Chapter 121

It seemed almost miraculous when, as the gloomy weather lifted, so did everyone's spirits. My babies smiled, Maria smiled, and Mila's thoughts turned to what she could wear over the weekend. "I only have things that hide a gun," she moaned.

I provided company funds to remedy her worry. Living alone in our small town was destroying her and I feared that she would jump ship. Any of our competitors would jump at the opportunity to hire away such a capable employee. If pushback came from the accounting department in Berlin, I felt sure that Vladimir would back my decision.

Feeling that we all deserved a Girl's Day Out, we shopped for Mila's clothes. Once again, Manhattan's Bergdorf Goodman was Erika's choice for this excursion. "We'll lunch in the 7th Floor restaurant. Their Gotham Salad is famous," she added.

"Erika manages things for her father too," I told Mila, as my way of apologizing for Erika's bossiness. Mila said nothing.

Erika, as she never fails to state, is "a serious shopper" and Mila's modest choices didn't satisfy her. Our purchases included a Kensington Belted Cashmere Long Trench Coat by Burberry ($2,690) and two dresses by Alexandre Vauthier whose designs Erika loves: a Puff-Shoulder Sheath ($3,115) and a Mini-Dotted Silk Wrap ($3,760). My anxiety increased even before Erika decided that Mila also needed the "essential accessories" of a Swiss cashmere-silk scarf, and perfume by Bottega Veneta.

Considering the last purchases more than a stretch, I quickly suggested that we go eat. Erika probably intends to buy Mila lingerie too though considering that she and the guy would have adjoining bedrooms, she shouldn't be wearing it long enough to matter, I thought.

Only Erika ordered the Gotham Salad. I chose the Scottish Salmon and Mila had the Roasted Black Cod. For dessert I ordered Strawberry Cheesecake, Mila had Gelato, and Erika had the Summer Peach & Sour Cherry Bread Pudding.

"This was a good day," Erika said, as Abram, her bodyguard-driver, held the door for us.

Mila's dancing eyes held the look of an expectant lover. It was a good day for the company too.

Chapter 122

Hoping to make things easier for me, Erika insisted that I and my babies stay at her house for the weekend too. We would otherwise be without personal security in Mila's absence. Apart from us, the group would be small: Erika's family, Mila, and Hans, the scientist.

Soon after arriving, I fed my babies. They cooperated by quickly falling asleep, leaving us free to talk.

"You've been edgier lately," Erika said.

"I am. The stress from the business and the group are adding up," I admitted.

"You must learn to let go."

"Being a boss means that you're *it*. Like an American President once said, 'the buck stops here.'"

"Try to relax this weekend," Erika pleaded.

She knows me well and her serious tone troubled me.

"I will. I just hope nothing else happens," I said.

There *were* no problems that weekend, which turned out to be delightful. Harry and Sarah virtually took over my baby-caring duties, practicing for the arrival of their baby in seven months. It had been a long time since a baby entered their lives. Mila, following her dating philosophy, downplayed her education and showcased her body.

After dinner, Erika whispered to me, "A hundred-dollars says it'll be five minutes."

"What will?"

"How soon she'll be naked after reaching her room."

"They did look intrigued with each other."

"Believe me," Erika said.

The bet caused me to wonder if this heavily protected home had video observation of the bedrooms too. Erika had done her best for Mila and Hans. The rest was up to them.

Chapter 123

"You're an angel!" I gushed to Erika.

"Well, maybe occasionally," she replied.

My son burbled happily as I continued.

"Mila and Hans were beaming at breakfast."

"I might have won the bet," Erika said, referring to her wager of how long it took Hans and Mila to jump into bed.

"That's another problem solved," I said, though with a downcast look.

"I'm worried about you. You're not usually like this," Erika said.

The words poured from me.

"I thought I knew everything from babysitting but never realized how helpless a newborn is. Caring for them is overwhelming and gripping. I'd thought that, with help, I could also work and go to school but their twenty-four-hour dependency and my lack of sleep wears me down. I'm amazed that I'm still alive when I wake up. My body works perfectly to meet their needs but mothering doesn't fit with the corporate life.

"I'm also battling the stay-at-home mother ideal which isn't me. I like working and planned to devote my life to meaningful work. Vladimir didn't force me to take this job. I enjoy helping people be safe."

"But you're a mother too," Erika said.

"Yes."

"When grown, your kids will be really something if they're like you," Erika said, with an approving smile.

"Maybe they'll take after Randy," I said.

I tried to smile but the thought of his failure to propose got in the way.

Chapter 124

"You should see Doctor Kandey again," Erika said.

Even though knowing that she was right, this wasn't what I wanted to hear. Doctor Kandey *is* sweet though many consider his name unfitting for a psychoanalyst. He had helped me when the confused feelings about my family popped up. This is understandable since, in addition to adoptive parents, I have a biological mother and *two* fathers who consider me their child. I might be either's since a DNA test was never done. Still, all love me and I love them and this is what really matters.

I gave in to Erika's concern.

"I'll call him," I said, and she changed the subject.

"Kira is happier now that she's spoken with her father," Erika said.

"*What? How?*" I cried.

"She sneaked her mother's phone and called him," Erika said, with a smile.

My depression vanished as I grasped my phone to call Krystal's bodyguard. Jason picked up on the first ring.

"*Meet me at midnight!*" I ordered.

"*Moving!*" he replied, and hung up.

Borya, my uncle, is a jolly person. Still, his nickname, Lucifer (The Devil), may explain why he holds high rank in the SVR, Russia's Foreign Intelligence Service. While helping to train me for a role in Vladimir's security business, Borya imparted important lessons. One was to always have a

Mayday code for an agent: a signal ordering them to drop everything and run for their life. I had just signaled Jason to take Krystal and Kira to a preset safe location.

After hanging up, I instinctively checked the Walther 9mm Luger PPS M2 pistol in my purse. Two spare clips rested there too.

"I must go. Can you watch my babies for a few hours?"

Erika instantly understood.

"Of course. But take Abram in an armored SUV," she said, grabbing her phone to call him.

I raced down the stairs and out the door to the waiting car.

Chapter 125

Abram accepted my odd destination without commenting. I felt guilty as the car left Erika's estate. While I had done well to advise Krystal's bodyguards of an emergency signal, I hadn't yet arranged for an alternate safe house.

Still, our meeting place should be safe though its broken gate and buried bodies wouldn't inspire confidence. The ancient Tomac Burying Ground, which is now next to a golf course on Tomac Avenue, was the first parcel of land bought from native Indians in 1640.

We arrived first. While waiting, Abram retrieved two suppressor equipped, 4.6X30mm/twenty-round, Heckler & Koch MP7 submachine guns from the compartments beneath our seats. After checking the magazines, he handed one to me. Five minutes later, a car sped into view as Abram watched through binoculars.

"They're alone," he said.

When it pulled alongside, Jason noted Abram warily.

"Abram is another of our bodyguards," I explained quickly.

They nodded toward each other as greeting. We had no time for small talk.

"Did you see anyone?" I asked.

"No. What happened?"

"Kari snuck her mother's phone and called her father. She might have told your location," I said.

"We got out quickly but they're terrified."

"I'll explain to Krystal. It would be best to get out of town. Stamford's Crowne Plaza Hotel would be good. It's bigger than the Delamar and the indoor pool will help them keep calm."

While Jason made the hotel reservation, I explained to Krystal.

"I'll talk with Kari and watch her better," Krystal said.

"There's an indoor pool at the new hotel. It'll keep her away from phones," I said.

"She'll never be out of my sight," Krystal promised.

Chapter 126

I closed my eyes and tried to relax as Abram drove us back to Erika's home. The already long day now seemed longer.

"It'll take time for the adrenaline rush to wear off. You won't be able to sleep," Abram said.

"For how long?" I asked.

"That depends. It won't be too many hours for you."

"You've known me a long time," I murmured, with eyes still closed.

"And your father longer," he said.

At the house, I rushed from the car toward Erika who held open the door.

"How are my babies?" I asked, apprehensively.

"Sleeping peacefully. I just checked them."

She steered me to the living room where I collapsed onto the sofa.

"You're worn out. You must slow down," Erika said softly.

"I can't seem to."

"You're good at caring for others but need caring too. You'll stay here tonight. I'll call Doctor Kandey."

I didn't need convincing and Erika persuaded Doctor Kandy to schedule my appointment on the following day. Upon entering his office, I felt as I had when we first met a year before. But now my life was far different even if I looked the same. I brought Doctor Kandey up-to-date.

"I dropped out of Barnard after giving birth to twins. I manage Vladimir's East Coast office with an assistant but can usually work from home," I said.

Doctor Kandey nodded. Like all skilled therapists, he only spoke when he had something useful to say.

"I need help," I said.

"It takes courage to admit it. You've never lacked that."

"Thank you," I said, with my first smile that day.

"Do you feel you can handle everything on your plate?"

"Yes, but the panic attacks which I had in the past have returned. Even the slightest sensation causes me to obsess that I'm having a heart attack and dying. It goes away when I get busy but then comes back. There's nothing medically wrong with me. How can I rid myself of this crazy thought?" I begged.

"You can't and wouldn't want to. A panic attack occurs when the normal symptoms of anxiety are incorrectly considered a deadly medical event. There is a war going on inside you which you must pay attention to.

"A panic attack is like a fever telling you that there's an infection, that something is wrong. When the infection goes away, so does the fever. It's the same with panic attacks which disappear when they're no longer needed. Our task is to figure out what's really bothering you," Doctor Kandey said.

Chapter 127

My anxiety disappeared upon hearing Doctor Kandey's explanation.

"I now feel great. You'd make a fortune bottling what you do," I said, with a real smile.

"That's what facts do. They remove fear by eliminating mystery. What's really bothering you: being a mother or your job?" Doctor Kandey asked.

"Neither. I'm handling both well. The anxiety seemed to begin after my talk with Randy."

"He's your children's father?" Doctor Kandey asked.

"Yes."

"Will you marry him?"

"I hope so but neither of us is ready."

"Were you ready to have children?"

"They were an accident but a good one," I said.

"How does Randy feel about being a father?"

"He's getting used to it and has always been good with kids. He'll soon graduate from Yale, to enter Columbia's doctoral program in Computer Studies."

"What about the talk bothered you?"

"It wasn't what he said but what he left out."

"What was that?"

"Marriage. He said he loves me but there are many fascinating women in Manhattan. I don't want to wind up a single parent," I said.

"You can make it on your own if you must."

"I don't doubt that but we've been together since I was thirteen and I don't want to lose him. We fit together. He needs a woman like me to manage his life while he does great science. He never got a haircut when his mother ordered it but always listened to me," I said.

"People can grow to resent those who provide what they need. It makes them feel weak," Doctor Kandey said.

"You're saying that he'll leave me no matter how much he values me?" I asked.

"Not if you talk honestly about it. Having good communication is the key to a lasting relationship. Looks fade but candid talk increasingly strengthens a couple's bond. Do you think that Randy would join us for a few sessions?"

Chapter 128

"How would it work?" I asked, cautiously.

"There would be no pressure. I'll speak alone with you for most of the session and then spend a few minutes with you both. I'll educate by telling stories about other couples and give each of you the opportunity to describe what frustrations exist. Of course, I couldn't tell Randy what you've told me. If there's an issue, either of you must raise it," Doctor Kandey said.

"How can I persuade him to come?" I asked.

"I've found that what works best with a treatment resistant husband is for the wife to suggest that his presence would help *her*. Stressing *she's* the sick one," he said, with a smile.

Before leaving, I scheduled another appointment for the following week. That night, I spoke with Erika. As a ten-year veteran of therapy, she has long been my expert on people's behavior.

"How do you intend to get Randy to Doctor Kandey's office?" she asked.

"Randy is coming for dinner tomorrow, after the kids are asleep. I'll raise the issue then," I said.

"Is he sleeping over?"

"He usually does."

"That's when I'd drop the bomb," Erika said.

"Couples counseling isn't a bomb," I insisted.

"It will be to him. Do whatever he likes sexually."

"I *always* do. *That* piece of advice I never needed," I said, in a firm but not nasty tone.

Chapter 129

"How did it go with Doctor Kandey?" Erika asked, a week later.

"It couldn't have gone better. Randy even reminded me of our next appointment."

"That must have been some sex you gave him," Erika said.

I gave her a look.

"What's doing with you?" I asked.

"I'm feeling so good that I'm suspicious," Erika said.

"As if waiting for the shoe to drop."

"Yep. Maybe I should talk in the group," Erika said.

"You're too normal."

"That's not what my boyfriend says."

"What does he say?"

"Never mind, I don't listen. All boys bitch and it's probably worse when they feel disabled."

"His diabetes?"

"Clarence feels it makes him less of a man though I continually tell him that he's my idea of perfect."

"Relationships are hard work," I said, as my child's crying interrupted our heart-to-heart.

"Back to mothering," I said.

"I'm pregnant." Erika said, softly.

"What?"

"It happens."

"Yes, but..." I sputtered.

"I know it's not the right time, with a pregnant step-mother. Will they throw me out of the house?" Erika asked, whimsically.

"Never, even though pregnant singles in wealthy families are rare in Greenwich."

"What about those who drop out of college too?"

"You're leaving school?" I asked.

"I hope to finish. Maybe take just a year off."

"One of us should set an example for our kids." I said.

"The internet has made it a different world. Who knows how it'll be when they're grown."

"Wouldn't it be something if one of mine married one of your's," I said.

"They wouldn't care but with us being like sisters, it would feel like incest to me," Erika said.

Chapter 130

After Krystal entered the Witness Protection Program, our company's involvement with her ended. One day she was here and the next day she was gone.

We had been close and she promised to keep in touch when this could be done safely. I gave her my secure e-mail address and suggested a secure e-mail provider for her.

The following weeks saw other changes too. Now, when not attending school, Erika spent more time at my home, seeking the tips that doctors don't ordinarily give to expectant patients. Like a mother's common fear when their infant breaks out with acne or they don't seem to respond normally to noises. Breast-feeding is best learned from an experienced friend too.

Nothing was rocket science and some she knew from her babysitting days. But that was with other people's children; caring for one's own is more emotionally challenging.

The group's discussion turned to children too. As Joanne's love affair deepened, marriage was discussed and the issue of when their kids should meet arose.

"Setting our wedding date is a snap compared to arranging a meeting for them," Joanne said.

Group outings were suggested but we couldn't really help. How the children meshed depended on their personalities of which we knew nothing. But we did our best, being supportive by listening which is sometimes all that a worried person wants.

"*You're* not using the group," Doctor Kandey said, when I described the meeting.

"No, I don't feel that I am," I said, after a brief silence.

"Why not?"

"Much that I do is confidential," I said.

"Not everything: worries about your children, your relationship with Randy, whether to return to college. These aren't business issues."

He was right.

Chapter 131

Doctor Kandey's suggestion was *partly* good. Sharing my concerns about meshing work with motherhood and whether to return to school would be OK but not my relationship with Randy. Doing so might cause a new problem.

I had spoken about him with Erika who doesn't gossip. But Jenna moved in our social circle and she would learn what I told the group. Considering her bitterness toward men, would she keep private what I revealed? Maybe, but I wouldn't take the chance. Nothing crashes a relationship faster than gossiping about it, my mother once told me, and about some things mothers do know best.

"I don't know what to do about school. Dropping out makes me feel a failure apart from the bad example it'll set for my children. But I feel overwhelmed managing both two infants and a job. I'm barely twenty but check for gray hairs daily."

My last line produced giggles and good advice from Joanne.

"Why not attend school part-time? Even if it takes six years to finish, you'll have done it."

"Barnard is in Manhattan and I hate driving in the City. Traveling by train and subway would take five hours on a good day," I said.

Jenna then spoke, so quietly that we all turned toward her.

"Phone the school, explain your problem, and ask that you be allowed to take as many classes as you can online."

"*Huh,*" I said, sensing this was a good idea.

"I'd add a twist to that," Erika said, with an impish smile.

I had seen that expression before. It was when she was had a particularly clever plan.

Chapter 132

"Phoning the school would make it easy for them to refuse. Make your request in person and I'll go with you," Erika said.

"That's nice of you, but..."

"Take your twins too," she added, interrupting me.

"My babies?" I asked, in a puzzled tone.

"Right. I'll hold one while you're talking to the dean, A pinch will make them cry and your plea irresistible," Erika said.

"That's brilliant!" Joanne said, as laughter arose.

"You're *not* pinching my baby!" I said, angrily.

"Of course not! But they'll agree when I say my father left Columbia's math department for Wall Street and would *love* to lecture Barnard students."

"Would he do it?" I asked.

"Yes," Erika replied, assuredly.

I didn't doubt it. Despite his complaints about her high-handedness, she had bought his clothes before his recent marriage.

"I'm sorry that we can't witness it," Sam said.

"We'll tell you everything," Erika promised.

I scheduled an appointment with Barnard's Dean of Studies. To avoid being late, I drove with my babies to Erika's house three hours before the meeting. Erika's bodyguard,

Abram, and Mila accompanied us. Caring for two fussing infants is a trial.

"Abram is happy to see Mila. He feared having to babysit them," Erika whispered, with a smile.

A traffic detour triggered by an accident caused us to take longer to reach Barnard. Abram left us at the building's entrance while he parked in a nearby garage.

Dean Smythe's warmth at taking Donna quickly changed to irritation upon hearing my plea. Silence filled the room and I saw her brain clicking. A single-parent dropout has *no* future at Barnard, she subtly communicated. It was as if I asked to change my major to pole dancing.

James began crying and I gave Erika a nasty look.

"Do you attend Barnard too?" Dean Smythe asked Erika.

"No, I go to Yale. They're considerate of my pregnancy, perhaps because of my father," Erika said.

"Your father?"

"Yes, you may know him too," Erika said, with a guileless expression.

She handed Dean Smythe her father's impressive business card.

"He taught math at Columbia before opening a hedge fund. He misses contact with students and when he heard that I was coming, told me to say that he would enjoy lecturing Barnard students on how America's economy can regain its traditional momentum. Margaret's father is a judge," Erika said.

The chilly atmosphere instantly changed into a love-fest.

"Margaret, it would *definitely* be possible to complete your degree online. The internet is education's future," Dean Smythe declared.

"She was sympathetic," I said to Erika, as we left the building.

"Don't you believe it. That was my money and your legal power talking," Erika said.

I dropped the subject.

Chapter 133

Being the mother of twins had worn me down. So, sitting at my laptop, I wrote The Home Rules to be followed by James and Donna when they entered First Grade. Number One was: Mommy works from home. *Do not* interrupt her unless you are bleeding.

Erika, who was holding James, looked down at what I wrote.

"You really are worn out," she said, sympathetically.

Vladimir phoned at that moment. When I hung up, a grin split my face.

"What?" Erika asked.

"Praise from Vladimir. He said that if I were in the military, I had just earned a battlefield promotion. Krystal told him that she would never forget me, that I had stuck by her when no one else did and she owes me her life."

"You can't get better than that. You'll never be happy as a stay-at-home mother. I brought you things to help get the rest you need," Erika said.

On the table lay a rectangular box holding a beige sleeping-mask from Kiki de Montparnasse and red Bottega Veneta pajamas.

"Thank you," I said, simply.

Erika is tremendously generous.

"You can cut off the buttons to make things easier for Randy," she said, playfully.

Feeling that a mother should be too mature to stick out her tongue, I gave her a stare.

"What are you working on now?" she asked, twenty minutes later.

"I'm trying to think outside the box. Why an event might not be true when everyone believes it," I said.

"That's the logic which my father counts on to make financial killings."

"It's a murder that I'm wondering about. Why would a nation kill an enemy at a location where blame would certainly be placed on them? It makes no sense," I said.

"It might have been done by a rogue agent after their country's leader thought out loud. Said they'd like someone dead but not actually ordering it."

"The deceased is being paraded as having been great though he had criminal contacts. The company has been offered a contract to discover what really happened but there's resistance to taking it."

"Because whatever answer you get, someone will hate you," Erika said.

"Exactly."

Chapter 134

Though loving my children, I quickly concluded what all mothers do: parenting is a mindless activity. Playfully babbling with kids is fun but only for a few minutes. Then comes their feeding and bathing accompanied by the continual worry whether they're achieving normal developmental marks for height, weight, and movement, and if what you saw is worth worry.

Having a live-in bodyguard who was also a physician provided comfort. But, Mila stressed, she had not been trained as a pediatrician and should not be relied on for medical advice.

Meanwhile, Erika supported me by simply being there, tolerating my increased horridness and unreasoning which made even me grow pale.

"You get like this when you're bored. You need a project to work on," she finally said.

This was true. Jordan was handling the office tasks and after Krystal left there was little for me to do. Thus, despite my hesitancy, I agreed to Vladimir's request to study the file describing Horst's life and death, which I had earlier mentioned to Erika.

Few, except his parents, ever said that Horst was nice. Though descended from a prominent German family he had, soon after college, entered the fast growing business of crime. Having been a computer prodigy since adolescence, he used his coding skill to enter the internet's Dark Web where drugs and weapons are sold anonymously using bitcoins.

Horst named his illegal marketplace *Roseland* and, as it grew, so did his wealth. His startup wasn't celebrated by all since governments were spending huge sums in their War on Drug Trafficking which Roseland enabled. Its trade in radioactive materials raised the stakes.

Nor were the drug cartels happy. While expanding the customer base for heroin and cocaine and meth and fentanyl, Roseland was taking away their customers. Why risk buying these unlawful products from a street dealer when one could safely do so online and have it delivered too?

"The real question is not why Horst was killed since many wanted him dead. But why the murder was committed where the motive seems obvious. Solve this riddle and the company will give you a bonus *and* pay for your children's education," Vladimir wheedled.

Chapter 135

"Why is the company even considering this job. We don't do criminal investigations?" I had asked Vladimir.

"You might say that it's a family matter. Borya asked for our help. Horst's death presents difficulty for Russia," he said, after a momentary silence.

Borya is my cherished uncle. Nicknamed *Lucifer* (The Devil), he is a highly ranked general in the SVR, Russia's intelligence service.

"*OK*," I said slowly, awaiting more information.

"Here, Russia's and America's interests coincide. The police of both countries are working together to take over the Roseland network. To convince buyers that they're dealing with Roseland whereas they're now dealing with government hackers. In this manner the identity and activities of buyers could be gained. Russia had no reason to kill Horst. They wanted him alive."

"So American and Russian interests *are* aligned?" I pressed, wanting to check what he declared.

"Absolutely or we wouldn't be involved."

"But if Russia is innocent, why are they concerned with Horst's death?" I asked.

"Because he was poisoned at Berlin's Russian Consulate." Vladimir said, and his voice took on an instructional tone.

"Russia has a long history of poisoning its enemies. The Grand Duke of Moscow was poisoned in 1453 with arsenic in

274

a chicken dinner, and in 1610 the Tsar ordered the poisoning of a Russian general which his wife did.

"But not only in Russia was poison favored. In 19th century France, arsenic came to be called *poudre de succession*, 'inheritance powder,' and was used by wives to rid themselves of husbands.

"In 1978, an anti-communist Bulgarian was poisoned with the tip of an umbrella containing a pellet of ricin. And you must have read of the recent attack in Britain."

I had. Sergei Skripal, a former Russian intelligence officer turned double agent, and his daughter, were poisoned by the nerve agent *Novichok* which causes cardiac arrest. Thankfully, both survived.

"Borya insists that Russia had nothing to do with Horst's death," Vladimir said, as if knowing what I was thinking.

"Do you believe him?"

"Your uncle wouldn't lie to me. Family is important to Russians," Vladimir said, in a chiding tone.

"I am sorry, but why have you asked me to work on this?" I asked.

"Because Borya believes that this crime can only be solved by thinking outside the box, as you did during Jenna's rescue," Vladimir said.

Chapter 136

Jenna, Erika's step-sister, had been kidnapped by a sex-trafficking gang. I theorized that these criminals needed a cooperating doctor to treat the captive women's sexually transmitted diseases and perform abortions. Pressuring him for information had enabled the women's rescue. I considered my idea to be ordinary but Borya considered it a stroke of genius.

Two days later, the package containing information about Horst's murder arrived. He and his girl-friend, Frieda, had entered the Russian consulate to get visas. She wanted him to meet her parents who lived in Moscow.

While completing the forms, Horst exhibited breathing difficulty and collapsed, dying before the ambulance arrived. The person nearest him was Frieda. Two consular clerks sat in another part of the room.

Though a routine autopsy found no evidence of poison, stories of Horst's "murder by Russia" were widely published. Considering where he died and Russia's long political use of poison, columnists insisted this had happened. I didn't, believing that no skilled assassin would be so dumb as to murder Russia's enemy inside its consulate.

In a Sherlock Holmes story was stated that when you eliminate all plausible possibilities, the remaining one, no matter how far-fetched, *must* be true.

Thus, when considering the death, two questions entered my mind. Who benefitted politically from Russia being blamed for the murder? And, considering that she was the person nearest Horst when he collapsed, exactly who was Frieda?

Margaret: Mother of Twins

My internet search quickly revealed the first answer. Elections would soon occur in Germany with close results expected. The major candidates had starkly different positions. One favored closer economic ties with Russia and eliminating the current European Union sanctions against it while the opposition favored no change. The murder by Russia of a man from a prominent German family could change the election result and the course of history. I trembled at the importance of my task.

Chapter 137

More newspaper headlines boomed "Murder" after a later, in-depth postmortem revealed that Horst was poisoned with a rare chemical, Batrachotoxin. Though chemically related to the plant-based Curare with which South American Indians tip their blowpipes to hunt prey, Batrachotoxin derives from the skin of tiny frogs.

"So deadly is this poison that an amount the size of two grains of salt will kill you. It interferes with sodium ion channels in the cells of muscles and nerves, jamming them open so they don't close and causing heart failure," the autopsy pathologist said.

Identifying Frieda proved difficult since she had disappeared. According to Horst's friends, they met a week before his death and he fell hard for her. Being a nerdy workaholic, he had only short-lived relationships in the past. His psychological autopsy contained interviews with several women that he dated. With his good looks and wealth, meeting them had presented no problem but courting them did.

Typical of the women's comments were: "He only talked about his work, even in bed," and "He would say nasty things like, when I was naked, 'Don't you shave?'" Considering this, Frieda's instant delight with Horst was more than puzzling since, by all accounts, she was ravishingly beautiful, an eleven on a scale of one to ten.

Seeking to check my inference, I raised the issue with my therapist, Doctor Kandey. While practicing in Washington, he had treated CIA operatives, still held a security clearance, and kept his mouth shut.

"I'm working on a puzzling case. Why would a gorgeous woman fall for a wealthy and handsome but nasty, socially inept man?" I asked.

"It happens. Money and good lucks can make up for many faults and women often believe they can improve their guy," Doctor Kandey said.

"OK. But what if he's murdered soon after they meet and she disappears?" I asked.

Doctor Kandey gave me an interested look.

"*That's* not usual," he said.

Chapter 138

Vladimir phoned me a week later.

"Frieda has been found," he said.

"Where?"

"In Manhattan. Her name is now Page."

"That doesn't sound Russian," I said.

"Borya is checking."

Another week passed before I heard more. Borya phoned early Sunday morning. His flight had just arrived from Moscow and we needed to meet. Could this be in Manhattan? He was expected in Washington and on a tight schedule.

I couldn't refuse though feeling torn since being with my babies was important too. But Borya was my uncle and, as Vladimir never tires of saying, family is important to Russians. I also knew that Borya would back me if I ever needed help.

I was picked up by a car flying a Russian flag and bearing diplomatic plates. The drive from Greenwich was comfortable and we met at the Russian Tea Room on West Fifty-Seventh Street.

If you've never been to this restaurant you should go. It's warm, cozy, and inviting, like a Russian amusement park out of history. It has red leather banquettes, golden samovars, chandeliers, period paintings, and shining green walls. The deep carpeting has a Russian motif, the ceiling glimmers with gold leaf, and the walls are accented with brass. Moreover, as

I discovered soon after arriving, the bathroom is spotless. As a new mother, I'd become obsessive about hygiene.

After a hug and inquiry about my children, Borya said, "We'll eat before talking."

Being a semi-vegetarian, I refused the Red Borscht (pickled red beets) because of its bacon broth and ordered the Grilled Salmon Bowl while Borya had Vareniki (Russian-style ravioli). For dessert I had the Vanilla Cheesecake covered with berries and he had the Chocolate Mousse Cake. His refusal of the waiter's suggestion of vodka, which the restaurant is noted for, indicated the importance of our meeting. The restaurant's opulence lent a solemnness to Borya's words.

"Page has dual American-German citizenship. Her story of wanting to visit her Russian parents is a fable. She was paid to seduce Horst and, we believe, to murder him. But we have no evidence and the public wants to believe the worst of us," Borya said.

I nodded understanding.

"Page now works for an escort service in Manhattan. We need someone to get close to her and thought of you," Borya said.

I nearly choked on my mouthful of cheesecake.

"*Me*?" I croaked.

Chapter 139

"You're beautiful and have worked undercover," Borya said, reassuringly.

"It nearly got me killed."

"But you survived."

"With you and Vladimir backing me," I said.

"We will now," Borya said.

"This is important?" I asked, rhetorically.

"It's vital."

"Then I'll do it."

Borya touched my hand.

"Why not? I've already pretended to be a babysitter in Tokyo and a pregnant fiancée in upstate New York. I could certainly be a whore in Manhattan too," I said, with greater humor than I felt.

"It won't be that. The owner of the escort agency is a Russian émigré with a family in Kiev. We've gained her cooperation," Borya said.

I gave him a questioning look.

"Have you seen the old movie, *The Godfather*?" he asked.

"Three times. I love it."

"What is its most famous line?" Borya asked.

I thought for several moments before answering.

"'I made him an offer he couldn't refuse,'" I said.

"Yes. Besides paying her well, we made her an offer she couldn't refuse. You'll live with Page but not go on escort jobs though she won't know this. To her, you'll be one of the girls."

Thinking of being absent from my babies, I asked, "How long will it take?"

"Probably no more than several weeks. We'll have a driver take you home to see your babies every few days. You'll tell Page that you've been hired by a rich businessman who's in town for a conference and is taken with you."

"It sounds like fun," I said, flatly.

There was no humor in my tone.

Chapter 140

I put down my fork, having lost my appetite for the admittedly wonderful cheesecake. Agreeing with Borya's request had thrown me. During my past undercover work I lacked a mother's tasks. Now, two babies needed me. Would my absence harm their growth? How could I prevent this? I asked myself.

"What's wrong?" Borya asked, noting my upset.

"I'm afraid."

"We have faith in your abilities," Borya replied.

""I'm afraid for my babies. I've never been away from them for so long," I said.

"Would you feel more comfortable seeing them daily?" Borya asked, after a momentary silence.

"*Absolutely*!" I said.

"Alright. We'll rent an apartment near Page's for your babies and hire a nurse to help Mila care for them. When Page is out working, you'll care for your babies. They'll sleep a lot and won't miss you at their age."

"That would work," I said grudgingly.

"I'm sorry. I never would have asked you if it weren't crucial. When your children are older, we'll give them a brilliant party in Moscow," Borya said, warmly.

A memory interrupted my gloom.

"I have good background for what you're asking," I said.

"How so?"

"My biological mother ran away from home as a teenager. After winding up penniless in Texas, she did office work at an escort service," I explained.

"Then you already know the business."

"Not enough to become Page's pal," I said.

"We'll have the agency's owner tutor you so you'll seem authentic," Borya said.

She did.

Chapter 141

Borya's staff worked rapidly. Within two days, an apartment was gotten and a nurse was hired. Would I care to inspect their fitness? I was asked. I would.

This time, in place of a flag-bearing limousine, an unremarkable white sedan drove Mila, me, James, and Donna to our temporary home. It was a luxuriously furnished four-bedroom apartment on the sixteenth floor of a new condominium. When I expressed surprise that the owner would be willing to rent it, I was told that he was Russian and had made it available without charge "in the interest of the state."

Premium infant furnishings would soon be delivered and be mine when my mission was completed. While I wasn't qualified to evaluate the nurse's skill, she related well to my babies and Mila approved her.

Feeling relief, I threw myself into learning how to be a whore. Some facts surprised me. I had believed that all hookers dress like those on innumerable TV shows, wearing miniskirts, skimpy tops, and larger-than-life makeup.

"Our employees look like well-dressed executives. They speak intelligently and have perfect manners. You would invite any to your wedding," Svetlana, the madam, insisted.

That might never happen considering Randy's hesitancy to propose, I thought, but just smiled.

"I should know some facts. What does a typical call girl earn?" I asked.

"Working on her own, a good one might earn three-hundred-dollars for a thirty-minute session. She would gain customers online or through referrals. My employees earn two-thousand-dollars an hour and see two or three clients a day for two to three hours each. Better than waitressing, isn't it?"

I couldn't help but nod agreement.

"Sharing stories will help me bond with Page. What bad experiences have your employees had?" I asked.

"Only one was *really* bad," Svetlana said, after several moments of thinking.

Chapter 142

"Nina was *so* beautiful: a statuesque blond with hair half-way down her back, twenty-six but looked like a high school cheerleader," Svetlana said.

"*Was?*" I asked, that seeming the operative word.

"She was murdered."

The story came slowly, it not being what Svetlana wanted to tell. Nina had arrived from Minneapolis with an Arts Degree, a hunger to live in Manhattan, and little money. While attending college, she worked as a waitress with a little hustling on the side, a trade which she entered accidentally.

"A restaurant's customer picked her up. After drinking at a bar, they went to his hotel room. He was in his thirties and attractive, an engineer attending a conference and looking for fun.

"She spent the night with him and after leaving in the morning, discovered that he stuffed three hundred-dollar bills in her purse. She stared at the money with amazement, having considered their night together to be a date and not a business arrangement.

"This happened during her last year of college. Things didn't go as she hoped in Manhattan. There were few jobs for Arts majors so she waitressed in one of the many restaurants that always have openings. Her pay was low and she shared a cheap apartment in a bad area until her roommate was slashed during a robbery.

"That decided her. She went online, searched for Escort Services, and settled on mine. She needed money and I paid far more than she could earn any other way," Svetlana said.

I nodded agreement.

"What happened to her?" I asked.

A tear rolled down Svetlana's cheek. Despite her dubious business, she is a good woman, I thought.

Chapter 143

"Nina was *so* beautiful," Svetlana repeated.

I again focused on the "was" and waited.

"Nina free-lanced though I'd warned her against it. But she was an independent soul and believed that she could take care of herself. Women always do until..."

I nodded.

"Her body was found handcuffed to the bed with her panties stuffed in her mouth. To muffle the screams, you understand."

My nod felt increasingly inadequate.

"They found our business card in her wallet and I had to identify her body. I cried when I saw her. She had been *so beautiful*," Svetlana said.

Being beautiful is often considered protective, I thought. Kimberly, my brother's fiancée, is beautiful too. Still, she had been imprisoned in the City's notorious Rikers Island Jail after being falsely accused of murder.

"I barely recognized her. The last joint of her fingers and toes had been cut off and the letter 'N' was cut into her chest and face. The pathologist said this was done when she was alive, that she died from blood loss and shock. The detective told me that her hotel room had looked like a slaughter house with blood everywhere."

"Was the killer caught?"

"It's still an open case. The police think he's a serial killer, that he's done this before and may have sought Nina because of something in their past. The extensive torture and carved initial indicates passion about an event, one possibly forgotten by her but important to him. Be careful with Page though she's not violent," Svetlana said, with a touch of concern.

"I'm bringing a friend," I said.

"A friend?"

"I never give an enemy half a break," I said.

I removed a small pistol from my pocket and held it palm up for Svetlana to see. It shone in the sunlight from the balcony.

Chapter 144

I was introduced to Page at Svetlana's office. As described, Page *was* an eleven on a scale of one to ten. She gave the easy confident smile of the beautiful as we faced across the table. They drank coffee while I drank mineral water, explaining that Mormons don't drink coffee. Page's smile broadened.

"I like that. Men will pay a lot for a religious girl with your looks but we *must* do something about your clothes. They're dull and make you look like a mother," she said.

How ironic, I thought, but said nothing. Keeping one's mouth shut is a good habit.

Svetlana told Page that we would be roommates and of her hope we would become close.

"What happened to Nina should be a wake-up call to everyone in the business," Svetlana said.

"Nina freelanced," Page said, matter-of-factly.

"Which is *not* a good idea!" Svetlana said, emphatically.

How otherwise could Page describe her involvement with Horst? I mused silently. The office phone rang and Svetlana waved us out. Male eyes lingered on Page as we walked Manhattan's streets.

Page's two-bedroom/two bathroom apartment was on the eleventh floor of a condo on West Fifty-Fifth Street. By craning my head on the balcony, I could see the building where my babies slept.

The furnishings were Danish Modern, the refrigerator was full, and the bed in my room was comfortable.

"There's linen in the closet opposite your bedroom and the cleaning woman comes on Mondays and Thursdays," Page said.

"Do you have clients here?" I asked.

"Never! None of them know where I live. My story is that I'm a scholarship student living in a dormitory. We meet at their hotel and payment is by credit card which Svetlana checks beforehand. She's careful and we're perfectly safe," Page assured me.

I would have crossed my fingers if I weren't a whore.

Chapter 145

I pretended to whore. Each morning I walked several blocks to the apartment where my babies awaited me. "If I only had breasts like yours," Page gushed, unaware that my impressive curves were milk factories.

Contrary to my fears, my babies thrived. They *still had* two playmates: Mila, and the pediatric nurse, Lee, who took my place. While I cuddled and fed them, she plied me with stories of other mothers.

"You're a natural. Some women never seem to get it," Lee said, and I couldn't help grinning.

"We're teaching them to say 'mama.' That'll come on your next visit," she said.

I kept my grin though being upset by the word "visit."

Days passed during which I learned no more about Page. We gossiped about girl things and she mocked her clients while I ridiculed my invented ones. It was while doing her nails, a skill which I had done on Erika throughout high school, that I got my first break. It arose from my idea as we munched popcorn and binged on *Designated Survivor*. This series describes the life of America's substitute president after a bombing in Washington killed many officials.

With a troubled expression, created by remembering when I barely escaped being murdered in Tokyo, I said, softly, "I've killed men."

Page didn't flinch or look away. She merely looked interested, as if I had spoken of a new push-up bra that I bought.

"You've killed men," she said, repeating my words and not enquiring if I was joking.

"Once was afterward. He tried to rob me and I gave him God's justice," I said, matter-of-factly.

Page studied me before speaking.

"We're going to be good friends," she said, in a thoughtful tone.

Chapter 146

Borya's deputy, Dimitri, was a tall, broad-shouldered man in his thirties. He spoke English without an accent, explaining that his grandmother had been a Londoner. His background sounded interesting but I never learned more. He had been sent to debrief me.

Dimitri listened closely as I cuddled my babies. He wanted the exact details of my conversations with Page and I did my best.

"Why did you make up that story about killing a man?" he asked.

"It wasn't wholly a lie. Not all snakes crawl on the ground," I said.

My vagueness was intentional but he instantly understood.

"I've heard that you're gifted, as you would being Vladimir's daughter and Borya's niece. You must come to Moscow," he said, with a broad smile.

"Perhaps, when my babies are older," I said, returning his smile.

"We need her confession on tape. Are there times when she's away so we can bug her apartment? We'd get better evidence and it would be safer than having you wear a wire," he said.

"I'll check her schedule with Svetlana. How long will you need?" I asked.

"Ten minutes, fifteen at the outside."

"I'll call you soonest." I said, using a term that I last used in high school.

Page *loved Designated Survivor*. The program's tension goosed her and she opened up, asking about my background and sharing her's.

"How old were you when you first had sex?" she asked.

"Twelve."

"That's young," she said, without surprise.

"It was my father. I killed him four years later," I said.

Something in my unconscious had told me to say this. "You have luck and good instincts. Trust them," Vladimir once told me. When I mentioned this to Borya, he modified the advice, "Being lucky is good but one shouldn't rely on it too often."

Page munched more popcorn before speaking again.

"My father waited until I was thirteen, after I got my period. I was beautiful even then," she said, smugly.

Chapter 147

I couldn't sleep that night, wondering why I had created the story of my father raping me. Why did I sense that telling this to Page would be productive? Then it hit me.

Many prostitutes experience incest as a child and harbor rage. It was likely that a woman who could casually murder a man hated them. Learning that we were both sexually abused and had killed might indeed foster a powerful bond.

It's a lousy job that I took on, I thought, trying to hold the vision of my innocent babies in my mind while falling asleep.

Upon entering my children's room the next day, I saw a stranger standing before my daughter's crib. He wore a pin-stripe, three-piece-suit and held the familiar doctor's bag.

"You must be Donna's mother," he said.

"Yes, what's wrong?" I asked, hurrying close.

"I'm Doctor Vlasov, a pediatrician. I was called to examine her when symptoms of a urinary tract infection surfaced: blood in her urine and low-grade fever. A urine specimen was cultured and confirmed my diagnosis. The infection is caused by bacteria from the stool and I prescribed an antibiotic," he quickly summarized.

My hand holding the door key hadn't stopped shaking.

"Cranberry juice helps prevent bacteria from sticking to the lining of the urinary tract. The nurse has gone out for some. You needn't worry. Feel free to call me whenever you're concerned. I've left my cell number," he said, before leaving.

Margaret: Mother of Twins

I calmed myself by breathing deeply. Mila touched my shoulder supportively.

"Donna will soon be fine. Her condition is common in girls," Mila said,

Despite her reassurance and knowing that every medical measure had been taken, I couldn't help feeling guilty. *I should have been with her!* I anguished.

Chapter 148

Mila and I were alone. The nurse hadn't yet returned from shopping for cranberry juice. I held James, stared at Donna, and feared that I was going crazy and not simply feeling mopey.

"It's hard for a parent when their child is ill. The feeling of helplessness," Mila said.

"It's not just that. Playing the spy game is wearying. Being friendly with a monster like Page eats at me. I feel that I'm losing my morality and becoming less human," I said.

"You're laboring for a good cause. Having America and Russia collaborate can only benefit the world, Speak to Vladimir. He's shrewd and it'll help," she said.

"I will. Vladimir *is* wise but in a way that I can't figure out. He has a far-reaching imagination and a natural ability to manipulate with flattery and persuasion. He's endlessly curious and speaks with a wide variety of people but superficially.

"One doesn't feel that they understand him or assume they're indispensable. Instead, one feels used, as if he is committed not to a person or even to a nation but to some hidden goal within himself which rises above the raging events of the day," I said.

"That's the best description of Vladimir I've ever heard and shows how close you two are. Call him. You'll feel better and he does love you," Mila said.

I did phone Vladimir. After describing my progress with Page and unease at not having been with Donna, his few words checked my despair.

"While not easy or painless, your work is crucial to maintaining peace in Europe. There is an innate human desire to be connected to something greater than themselves. Each person has their own Great War and this may be your's."

A later phone call gave me another explanation why I felt poorly.

"It is when we feel most unloved that we need reassurance. It wasn't Vladimir's comforting that you needed but Randy's,' Erika said.

Chapter 149

As usual, Erika was correct. Randy's indecisiveness *had* gotten to me. His educational goal and career were certain. I owned a house, had a well-paying job and more than enough money for our family to live comfortably. So why doesn't he propose? I kept asking myself.

True, his dating experience was limited, I having been his only girl-friend. His one affair consisted of a sexual contact when he was drunk and he never saw the woman again. And, like me, *she* had sought *him*. Randy seemed to fall for assertive women no matter how much he resented their actions.

I wanted to mull over my quandary longer but duty called. Page's apartment had been wired and our relationship required burnishing. She would return late and I would have dinner ready. If I were really a whore, we would make a good working couple, I thought.

While I'm careful what I eat and long regarded sugar and fried foods as toxic, Page didn't. Before we met, she ate lousy with fast-foods predominating. Burgers, fries, and milkshakes were her usual lunch and dinner; popcorn was her healthiest food. Her fare nearly made me gag. Thus, though not part of my assignment, I wound up cooking for us.

My meals were simple but healthy: yogurt, oatmeal, and fruit for breakfast; baked fish, vegetables, and whole-grain breads for dinner; and more fruit, cheese, milk, and yogurt for snacks. When Page objected, I added granola bars containing the least sugar. Thanks to this change of diet, Page felt better and we became closer.

"We fit together well, like we were made for each other," she gushed, warmly.

Chapter 150

Weeks passed without development. Donna's rapid recovery dispelled *that* worry but others remained. I felt a sense of suspended animation as the anxiety of living a double life wore me down. I was impatient to end my mission, to return to Greenwich and a normal life.

I hadn't spoken with Randy since leaving Greenwich, not being free to explain my activity. He would have gone ballistic, particularly since our children were indirectly involved. So I had told him that we would be visiting my relatives in rural Utah where the Wi-Fi connection was spotty.

Earlier written letters, affixed with a Utah postmark, were regularly mailed, accompanied by cheery photos of James and Donna. His replies were forwarded to me. He would finish his Yale degree early, and had a good meeting with his future doctoral adviser at Columbia University.

One letter closed with a plaintive cry written in block letters: "I MISS YOU!" "I miss you too, love," I said aloud, kissing his letter before destroying it. It was too risky to carry to Page's apartment.

My edginess aroused revulsion toward Page which I found increasingly hard to stifle. Hoping to conceal this feeling, I cooked elaborate meals and behaved more caring of her needs.

"Will this never end?" I moaned to Mila, my only nearby support.

"Soon, and I'm sure you'll have a splendid career. You have a natural talent for taking advantage of human weakness which is the core of spying," she said.

"I'm hoping for a long life too. I don't want my children viewing my memorial and asking one another, 'Do you remember mama?'"

Mila smiled.

"Things often get better just when you feel you can't take more."

She was right-on.

Page came home earlier that evening. I was busily baking apple tarts, following the recipe from a cookbook that I bought that day. Hearing multiple footsteps, I turned with flour-spattered hands.

A tall muscular figure of about forty stood beside Page. Despite hooded eyes that made him seem half-asleep, he radiated power.

"Franz wants to meet you," Page said, coldly.

She didn't look happy.

Chapter 151

"Margaret. May I call you Margaret?" Franz asked, politely.

"Sure. I just have to get these in the oven," I said, turning away.

After rinsing and drying my hands, I turned toward them. They were sitting at the dining room table and I sat opposite.

"Does anyone want something to drink?" I asked, assuming the role of hostess.

"Thank you, no," Franz said.

His speaking for both was meant to show *he* was the boss.

"Page has told me about you," he said.

"All good, I hope," I said.

I tried to make my smile authentic despite my anxiety.

"Some that's bad but good for our work," Franz said.

"Huh?" I exclaimed, still using the childish expression which I hadn't yet outgrown.

Franz smiled.

"I don't understand," I said.

"Page has told me of your murders," he said calmly.

I gave Page a dirty look which Franz noticed.

"It was done with your best interests in mind. She values your friendship and believes that you could work together."

"Svetlana would object," I said.

"The jobs would be infrequent and she needn't know," Franz said.

"I don't understand," I repeated, hoping to seem innocent.

In the past, I had found that playing dumb could be useful.

"I manage a *problem elimination business,* removing difficulties permanently. You two could work together."

"*I see,*" I said, slowly.

"Yes. Like the Berlin consulate murder you may have read about. He was a problem."

"And this work pays well?" I asked.

"Very well since our clients are grateful. Some jobs require a wingman," Franz said.

I couldn't help smiling at this dating term being used to refer to murder.

"How much could I expect to earn?" I asked.

Greed should seem my strongest motive.

Franz turned toward Page.

"How much were you paid for the Horst job?" he asked.

"Four-hundred-thousand dollars," she said.

"That would likely be your minimal fee. The job's difficulty governs how much it pays," Franz said.

"Of which you get a cut," I said.

"A small one," he agreed, with a smile.

I extended my hand.

"We have a deal," I said.

Page, my new business partner, didn't look happy.

Chapter 152

After Franz left, I turned toward Page.

"What's wrong?" I asked.

"It's Franz, not you. We're an item and I saw how he looked at you," she said, angrily.

"Don't worry! It'll always be just business between us. I'll cut off his dick if he pulls it out," I said, brandishing the kitchen knife.

Page's laugh showed that we were still friends.

"While I hold him down," she said.

Trading on our camaraderie moment, I asked a crucial question.

"How did you manage to poison the man in the consulate without being seen by the officials?"

"That *was* creative! The poison was on my gloved hands which he kissed. I quickly discarded them and no one noticed," she said.

"*Clever girl,*" I said, admiringly.

Page beamed with satisfaction.

"We make a good team," she said.

"Yes," I said.

We munched on the apple tarts.

"These are *really* good," Page said.

Not as good as your videotaped confession, I thought.

Despite my success, I felt a surprising sadness the next day.

"What's wrong?" Mila asked.

"I don't know. The authorities now have what they need and Franz and Page are goners. But for some irrational reason I feel sorry for her even knowing how awful she is. I mean, she's an assassin," I said.

"That's how it sometimes is. You've shared ordinary things and bonded. The difference is that you're on the side of the angels. But I wouldn't shed tears. German prisons are humane and she may never see one," Mila said.

"How could that be?" I asked.

"By telling a convincing, tear-filled story and turning on Franz. She's an exceptional assassin and many nations would value her skill," Mila said.

"Even Borya?" I asked, with astonishment.

"I wouldn't bet against it. There are always rattlesnakes to crush," she said.

Mila was correct.

The world quickly lost interest after learning that Horst's murder had been an ordinary drug-gang killing. Doing it in the consulate was a ruse to make his murder appear political. Five months later, I asked Vladimir, "What happened to Page?"

"Ah, the beautiful Page lives in Moscow. Borya says that she asks about you and is assured that you are doing well too," he said.

"And Franz?"

"He's dead. While awaiting trial in Berlin, he was knifed in the street by a mugger who was never identified. The authorities explain it as a robbery gone wrong. How sad. And Berlin was once so safe," Vladimir said.

I dropped the subject.

Chapter 153

My support group became smaller after Vladimir's investigation revealed that, rather than being a terrorist, Sam's landlord was employed by the Department of Homeland Security. Her pistol and interest in college students and explosive devices were part of her job.

Upon learning this, a relaxed Sam left the group after profusely thanking us. Things were going well with Joanne's boyfriend and Vera was hopeful about a man whom she met online. With these developments, our discussions became ordinary and Erika joined in.

"My new family is Finnish," she began, looking at Jenna.

"Is that bad?" Jenna asked, seeming hurt.

"No, I didn't mean that. I love you all and bless the day you entered my life. Cultures make people different, not better or worse. But I don't understand why Finns never seem to talk to each other," Erika said.

Jenna relaxed, sat back in her chair, and took a sip of coffee.

"Finns *are* different. They don't believe in talking bullshit," she said.

"Huh?" I burst out.

Jenna smiled.

"It's not to insult other cultures. Finns spend hours talking about serious stuff like sex or politics but don't believe in casual conversation. A national saying is, 'Silence is gold, talk is silver.' There's no small talk even with close friends. A popular Finnish saying is that the foreigner is the loudest person on public transport.

"It may seem strange that a people who feel comfortable getting naked in a sauna with a stranger can't talk to them on a bus but that's us. We even have classes teaching how to chit-chat by giving safe topics to talk about. Students practice by play-acting meeting someone for the first time. Finns find this painful," Jenna said.

Erika smiled, reached over and touched her hand.

"That's reassuring. I thought you didn't like me," she said.

Chapter 154

When the group's discussion consisted of shopping recommendations, I concluded that its usefulness had ended.

"The group has helped us but I sense that it's time is over. Raise your hand if you disagree," I said.

No one raised their hand.

"OK. I suggest that we end with a party," I said.

There were no objections and I left its arrangement to Erika. Creating parties had been second-nature to her since high school.

Its food was mostly our usual: baked salmon, sliced turkey, cheeses, and breads to make sandwiches. But in place of our usual desserts, there was a huge oatmeal-raisin cookie for each to take home. Written on it in vanilla frosting were our names and the words, "Sisters Forever." Mine weren't the only tear-filled eyes in the room.

When the others were gone, I sat alone with Erika.

"I finally feel relaxed. The past months were a nightmare."

"You've been through a lot. Now you can return to a normal life."

"My life was never normal."

"That's true and being a mother has sent you on an additional path. Go to Barnard one day a week. It'll keep you grounded," Erika advised.

"I don't know about that. The other students will gossip about clothes and I'll be worried about vaccinations. We inhabit different worlds. I'd be a wounded soldier amongst shoppers," I said.

"That's a good image except for being wounded," Erika said.

"I am inside," I said.

Being as close as sisters, we sense when arguing is futile. My healing would take time but I was young.

www.Ingramcontent.com/pod-product-compliance
Lightning Source LLC
Chambersburg PA
CBHW020436270626
47155CB00022B/496